I go over to my computer and pull up Google. I type in *Santa Monica* and the word *attack*. A second later, a news item pops up. The headline makes my jaw drop:

SURFER FOUND ON SANTA MONICA BEACH WITH SEVERE NECK WOUND; IN STABLE CONDITION AT HOSPITAL.

"Oh no," I whisper.

I shrink backward in my chair, terror gripping my throat. There's no way this is a coincidence. Somehow I feel responsible; as if I should have done something to prevent this. As if I need to do something now.

I glance wildly around my room. I could call the police, but then I'd run the risk of everyone discovering I'm a vampire. I could — I could — I close my eyes, overwhelmed. Then, in the next instant, there's nothing I can do.

Because I'm transforming into a bat.

POISON APPLE BOOKS

At First Bite

by Ruth Ames

SCHOLASTIC INC.

New York   Toronto   London   Auckland
Sydney   Mexico City   New Delhi   Hong Kong

ISBN 978-0-545-32487-8

12 11 10 9   14 15 16/0

Printed in the U.S.A.   40
First printing, November 2011

For Noah and Margot,

who are always perfect

to me

Chapter One

There are a few myths about vampires that I should clear up, right from the start.

Myth #1: Vampires are waxy and pale.

This is totally untrue. Take me, for example: Ashlee Samantha Lambert. My skin is rosy and glowing (helped along by blush sometimes, but whatever). With my long blond hair, glossed lips, and skinny jeans, I appear to be a perfectly normal twelve-year-old girl. I hope.

Myth #2: Vampires drink blood.

Um, ew? Okay, yes, there are *some* of us out there who hunt small wild animals for this purpose. But thankfully my amazing vampire mentor, Arabella, told me about Sanga!, a refreshing blood substitute drink that comes in these adorable frosted cups with rounded lids, like Frappuccinos. Sanga! was invented by a genius vampire who was as grossed out by hunting as I am.

Myth #3: Vampires sleep in coffins.

No way. I sleep in my white canopy bed, high above the streets of Manhattan. Of course, now that my family's moving to Los Angeles, I'll no longer be able to see skyscrapers from my pillow, but I guess I'll see the ocean instead. Not a bad trade-off, and much better than staring up at the velvet lining of some creepy coffin. Obviously.

Myth #4: Vampires turn into bats.

All right . . . this is, well . . . this actually seems to be the case. At least, in my limited experience. It's how we're meant to hunt (if we have to) or hide from the prying eyes of non-vampires. The problem is, I stink at bat-shifting. You have to visualize wings sprouting from your body and fangs shooting out of your mouth — and then presto, you're transformed. Instead, I start to transform when I *least* expect it, like in the middle of a stressful math exam. Then I have to dash to the nearest bathroom and wait to shift back. It's horrifying — worse than split ends *and* chipped nail polish combined.

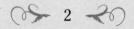

This is what I'm thinking about tonight as I'm packing up my bedroom with my best friend, Eve Epstein. I'm cramming books into a box and praying that I won't suddenly feel my ears going all long and pointy. I reach up and touch them to make sure. My teeny diamond studs are still there, so I let out a relieved breath.

"What are you *doing*?" Eve demands from across the room. She's standing on my desk in her wedge booties, removing the Christmas lights I'd strung across the wall. It's already January, but I forgot to take them down. "I asked you the same question, like, three times now."

"Oh, sorry," I say, blinking. "I was wondering — um, if there'll be enough space for all my clothes in my new bedroom."

Eve doesn't know the truth about me. No one does. Not my mother, not my brother. No one.

Well, there *is* one girl from school who knows. We were never friends (she's not in the popular crowd, even though she's now sort of dating the cutest boy in the grade), but she swore to keep my secret. Still, I've been terrified she might tell someone. At least in my new school, I won't have to avoid her in the hall-way anymore. Whew.

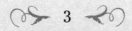

"I was *asking*," Eve says impatiently, "if you think you'll get to be on TV." She hops off my desk and flops onto my bed, her brown ponytail bouncing.

I bite my lip to keep from laughing. Or maybe crying.

My mom is going to be on her own reality show, *Justice with Judge Julia*. That's why we're moving to LA. But there's no way I'll ever be on TV. I don't show up in photographs or on film. (Another vampire myth that is, sadly, true.) I learned that the hard way in November, when I tried to iChat with my other BFF, Mallory D'Angelo, and all she saw was my desk chair. Luckily, Mallory isn't too sharp, so she bought my explanation about the computer being broken.

"Probably not," I answer, fighting down the lump in my throat. I'd always dreamed about going to Hollywood and being picked to star in a movie. "You know I don't like to be on camera anymore," I add. "Not since I got self-conscious about my eyebrows." That's the explanation I've come up with for Eve. (In truth, I like my eyebrows just fine.)

"That's right. You're such a weirdo," Eve giggles

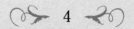

as she reaches across the bed for my laptop. From where I stand, I can see my screen saver, which is a slideshow of all the pictures in my iPhoto album. There I am: giving my acceptance speech as student council president; posing next to the cupcake tower at my birthday party, surrounded by dozens of admiring faces; trying on a dress at Bloomingdale's that every girl in school wanted the next day . . . all reminders of the way things used to be.

Don't get me wrong. I'm still popular. I shudder to think what *not* being popular would be like (worse than surprise bat-shifting, possibly). But it's undeniable that everything in my life has changed.

It all started when I turned twelve, back in September. My teeth began to hurt, like they were growing, and I came out blurry in photographs. Then, one rainy night in October, I received a personalized, crimson-colored invitation . . . to my vampire initiation ceremony. The invitation explained that my great-great-grandmother on my mother's side had been a vampire from Transylvania. Apparently, I had inherited this secret trait, and the invite said I could tell no one about my "condition."

Of course, I freaked out. I almost told Eve and Mallory, but I knew they'd think I was crazy. So I went to the ceremony on my own. There, I was joined by many other frightened twelve-year-olds from around the world. The Empress of Vampires recited an incantation and we all bat-shifted for the first time. Then we followed older vampires — also in bat form — into Central Park as they hunted down small wild creatures. The things I saw and heard that night still send shivers down my spine two months later.

"Are you sure you don't want to come to Mallory's tonight?" Eve is asking me now as she checks her e-mail. "It's the party of the year."

"The year just started," I remind her drily, but she doesn't look up at me.

Mallory is hosting an End of Winter Break bash at her apartment, and, as the invite said, *Everyone who's anyone will be there!* Mallory blatantly stole that line from an old slumber party invite of mine. So I don't really feel like going.

The thing is, I've sort of been avoiding parties — and people — ever since I became a full-fledged vampire. My skin is cold to the touch, so I duck away from hugs. All my senses are heightened: Kids look at me like I'm nuts when I can smell what's for lunch a mile from the cafeteria. I got so paranoid about hiding my ginormous, creepy secret that I even resigned as student council president (Eve immediately took my place). And I started spending more time in my room and less time shopping, so I lost my title as fashion queen. In December, when Mallory wore little woolen shorts over her tights, all the girls copied *her* look.

That's why I'm actually excited about moving across the country. In California, I can make a fresh start. I'll be the new, cool girl from New York City. I'll be back on top in no time at all. I can't wait.

"You've gotten so lame." Eve sighs, echoing my thoughts as she snaps my laptop shut. "It's your last night here!"

I narrow my eyes at my friend, wishing she could understand. I feel a twinge of self-pity. I didn't *ask* to become a vampire, but here I am, stuck in this sorry situation.

"Well, I need to finish packing," I argue as I shove the last book into the box.

The other reason I'm hesitant to leave is that I'm suddenly super-thirsty for some Sanga! I still eat regular food, but if I go too long without Sanga! I get shaky and weak.

"Whatever," Eve scoffs, standing up. Then she

freezes, and her brown eyes widen. She points right at me. "Wait. Is that — is that . . . a *bat*?"

My stomach turns to ice. *No.* I'm too scared to touch my arms and see if they're becoming leathery wings. *This can't be happening!* I think, panic rising in my throat. *Not in front of Eve, when she's about to go to the party of the year, and I'm —*

"Behind you!" Eve says, pointing emphatically. "Outside! Gross!"

Knees shaking, I turn to look out my window. The bone-white moon glows between the snow-dusted apartment buildings. Then I see it — a quick, dark shape darting past my window again and again, as if impatiently pacing back and forth. It takes me a second to recognize the distinctive red markings on the wings. I shake my head in disbelief. It's my vampire mentor, Arabella. Why would she show up unannounced?

"I think it's just a bird!" I blurt, too loudly, whipping around and pressing my back against the cold window. "A bat-bird. I did a project on them in science class. They're all over the city."

Eve squints at me suspiciously. I swallow hard, waiting for her to nudge me aside and throw open the window to see for herself. But I guess she's gotten used to me acting like a lunatic, because after a minute, she shrugs.

"I should get over to Mallory's anyway," she says, giving me a quick hug. "Ooh, you're always freezing," she adds, pulling back and shuddering. "I guess this is bye."

"Yeah, bye, I'll text you from LA," I babble, waving. I thought that Eve and I would have a tearful, extended farewell. But now I want her to leave as quickly as possible. I can practically *feel* Arabella hovering outside.

With another questioning glance in my direction, Eve takes her coat and slips out of my room, closing the door behind her. I wait until I hear her say goodbye to my mom and brother in the kitchen. Then I spin around and yank open my window, letting in a blast of frigid air.

"Arabella!" I hiss, and she appears, flapping her wings innocently. "*Eve* was in here! Why didn't you call first?"

Arabella flies into my bedroom, zipping past my ear. I slam the window shut and by the time I've turned to face her, she's transformed. Her red curls tumble down her back, and her platform pumps make her look even taller than she already is.

"I'm on a serious deadline, Ash," Arabella explains, smoothing out a crease in her black cashmere poncho. "But I wanted to see you before you leave tomorrow."

Arabella Lowe was assigned to be my mentor the night of my initiation ceremony. All young vampires get a mentor — a guide who can help them through this strange new world. I feel super-lucky that I got paired up with Arabella. She's only twenty-five, but she's an editor at a top fashion magazine, which is what I'd like to be someday. I only wish Arabella had more time to spend with me; she's always busy attending runway shows.

"Oh — thanks," I say, softening, and Arabella grins at me. "I'm going to miss you so much," I admit, heading to my closet to get a Sanga! "Are you sure there's no way you can come to California with me?"

Arabella sighs. "Honey, you know I'd love to. But I have my work and my family here, and Beau, too." Beau is Arabella's boyfriend, another vampire, and he's totally dreamy. "You'll be *fine* without me," she adds. "Better than fine. Besides, we'll e-mail."

"And text," I agree, pulling the red-and-white cooler from the back of my closet.

Sanga! has to remain at a certain temperature to stay fresh, so it comes in special insulated cups that you have to store in a cooler. Luckily, Arabella gave me the hot new vampire must-have: a Sanga! mini-cooler that I can carry in my schoolbag. She ordered it from the Sanga! online store. Only vampires have the password to the site, and we can order a six-month supply at a time.

I pluck out a container filled to the brim with bright red liquid: The drink looks so much like blood that it's best to sip it in private. I stick in a straw and take a long, quenching gulp. *Ahh*. Delicious. Right away I feel a surge of energy.

"But listen, Ash," Arabella says, her tone growing serious. I glance up and see that her green eyes have darkened with concern. "I also came to warn you about something."

Fear makes the back of my neck prickle. I shut the cooler and get to my feet. "Warn me?"

Arabella nods. "I've been hearing rumors that" — she takes a breath — "Dark Ones are hiding in Los Angeles."

I must look confused, because before I can even ask, Arabella says, "I'm sorry, Ash — sometimes I forget you still have a lot to learn." Then she pauses, glancing at my closed door. As a more experienced vampire, Arabella has even sharper hearing than I do; it takes me a few seconds to hear my mom's footsteps coming down the hall.

"She's probably going to the bathroom to apply her rejuvenating clay mask," I whisper, eager for Arabella to continue.

Arabella nods. "Dark Ones are vampires who bring shame upon the rest of us," she whispers back. I feel small tremors down my spine. "They shun Sanga! and they don't drink the blood of small wild creatures. No, Dark Ones, like the vampires of long, long ago, are only content with one thing: drinking human blood."

My heart is pounding in my throat and I set down my Sanga! on the dresser. "That's disgusting," I whisper. "And awful. But they can't hurt *me*, can they?"

"No, but they are very dangerous," Arabella whispers back. "And —"

"Ashlee!" a voice calls outside my door.

Uh-oh.

It's my mom. She must have decided the rejuvenating clay mask could wait.

Arabella and I exchange frantic glances. How will I explain Arabella's presence in my bedroom? Or the

Sanga! on my dresser? Mom has already asked me about "that red drink" she once saw me with. And then there was the time I was midmorph and she glimpsed my fangs and asked me if I needed a special orthodontist appointment.

"I should get out of here, Ash," Arabella says, hurrying over to the window. "But text me if you encounter anything suspicious, okay?"

Mom is turning the doorknob. I look from the door back to Arabella, my palms growing clammy. I don't want my mentor to leave yet. I still need to know more.

"Like what?" I whisper as Arabella pulls up my window, the night wind catching her curls and blowing them in all directions. "What sort of suspicious —"

"Ashlee Samantha!"

Suddenly, my mom is in my room, hands on her hips, and I have just enough time to knock my Sanga! into the trash basket behind me . . . *and* to see a bat take flight from my windowsill. I watch its shape as it sails off into the night.

"Were you talking to someone?" Mom demands. But before I can invent a fib, she moves on to a new topic. "Why is your lipstick on like that?"

"Wha — I —" I glance at the mirror over my dresser. (Thankfully, the myth about vampires not showing up in mirrors is a false one.) Horrified, I see that some Sanga! is smeared around my mouth. I brush my hand quickly over my lips, and Mom nods approvingly. She always likes everyone to be as neat and pretty as she is.

My mother has big blue eyes and silky blond hair that she wears cropped short. She says we look alike, which makes me happy, but she says I have my dad's chin, which I'm not sure is a good thing. I don't know my dad very well: He and Mom divorced when I was little, and he lives in London. For as long as I can remember, it's been me, Mom, and my older brother, Dylan, (and a rotation of nannies) living in this apartment. Mom was working as a big-shot judge downtown when she got the call from Los Angeles about the reality show. She agreed immediately: Mom loves the idea of a fancy, famous life. I'm sure having a vampire for a daughter doesn't fit into that plan.

"It's time for dinner," Mom says, motioning to the door. "I ordered sushi — your favorite."

"Yum," I say halfheartedly; I wish I'd finished my Sanga!

As I follow Mom out of my room, I glance back at my bare walls and stack of boxes. It's crazy to think that the movers will come first thing in the morning, and then Mom, Dylan, and I will board an airplane.

I feel a tingle of excitement — but then a chill of worry. Arabella's warning lingers in my mind. I'll have to ask her more about the Dark Ones as soon as possible. Otherwise, her words will continue to haunt me.

Chapter Two

"Check out all the palm trees!" Dylan shouts the next day, rolling down the window of the airport taxi. *"Sick!"*

I roll my eyes. "Stop trying to sound cool, Dylan," I groan. My fifteen-year-old brother is a major dork. I'm talking computer obsessed, no social skills, bad dresser. If it weren't for his blond hair and blue eyes, I'd swear we weren't related.

But for once, I have to agree with him. Los Angeles is gorgeous. We're zooming down a wide boulevard lined with tall green palms. The sky is cloudless, the air smells like flowers, and the sapphire ocean shimmers to our left. I let out a happy sigh. Arabella's unsettling visit last night has slipped my mind.

"This area is called Santa Monica," Mom explains from the passenger seat. "And this," she adds as the cab comes to a stop, "is our new home."

"Seriously?" I gasp. The house is big and cream colored, with a wraparound balcony. It looks, as Dylan would say, pretty sick.

"Seriously," Mom laughs while Dylan whips out his iPhone and starts tapping away at the screen. I have no idea what he's doing, but I don't care. I'm in California! I burst out of the cab with my heavy duffel bag. The bright sunshine warms my shoulders, and I can't wait to change out of my cords and turtleneck sweater.

After the driver unloads our luggage, we straggle up to the house and Mom unlocks the front door. As we step inside, I'm surprised by the sudden, hushed emptiness. Cobwebs dangle from ceilings, and a lonely shaft of sunlight slices the living room walls. Long, twisting hallways lead to dark corners. It's a little spooky, and I shiver.

"Hey, check it," Dylan says, holding up his iPhone. "I looked up the address online, and it turns out a movie was filmed in this house ages ago! A *horror* movie."

"Really?" I ask, my stomach tightening. No wonder

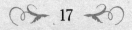

the inside feels ominous. I can almost hear the faint echoes of screams, and I can picture a beautiful actress fainting by the doorway. . . .

"Yeah, it was called *At First Bite*," Dylan says, glancing at the screen. "So cool! Mom, why didn't you tell us?"

"Whatever," I snap. "It's not cool, it's *creepy*." When you're basically *living* a horror movie, you don't want to have anything to do with one. I've never heard of *At First Bite*, but the sound of it makes my teeth throb. I hope I won't feel a fang start to form.

Mom shakes her head as she sets down her suitcase. "Don't be ridiculous," she tells me. "A million different movies have been filmed in a million different homes here. I know the space is unfamiliar now, but when our furniture arrives and we put down rugs, it'll be *perfect*."

Perfect is my mom's favorite word. I like it, too. And I know she's right. I was just being silly, getting weirded out by the new place. It's time to relax and settle in. As if reading my mind, Mom tells Dylan and me to go upstairs and unpack.

"Okay, but I get dibs on the bigger bedroom!" Dylan hollers as he thunders up the stairs, the frayed laces on his Converse flapping.

"You're pathetic!" I yell after him, but I follow close behind, my duffel bag swinging from my shoulder.

Dylan grabs the first room off the stairs, so I end up with a more private one down the hall. Best of all, it has a floor-to-ceiling window that opens up onto the balcony. I smile and step outside, and I see that I'm facing the beach. My heart leaps. Golden sand, crashing waves, and, in the distance, a Ferris wheel. I can see kids in shorts, carrying boogie boards and laughing.

And I know what I have to do.

I hurry back into the room, kneeling down to unzip my duffel bag. When I start my new school tomorrow, I will have the world's best tan.

Ten minutes later, with Mom's permission, I am flip-flopping across the sand in my pink bikini, a towel tucked under one arm. The beach is crowded, which is no surprise. It's a Sunday, and according to Dylan (and the weather app on his iPhone), unseasonably warm for mid-January. People are dozing in loungers or playing volleyball

When I find an empty spot, I spread out my towel, lie down, and breathe in the salty air.

Ahh.

This is heaven. It's been about eight hours since I left cold, slushy New York, but it feels like a lifetime ago. *Maybe*, I think recklessly as I stretch my arms over my head, *I won't even* be *a vampire here anymore. Maybe everything that happened in New York was like a bad dream.*

After all, who can dwell on things like bats and blood when the sun is this strong and seagulls are cawing overhead? I'm not even craving the Sanga! that's stashed in one of my suitcases back at the house.

Not really, anyway.

I take my cell phone out of my bag and text Eve and Mallory:

Arrived in LA. Lying on the beach. JEALOUS?

Grinning, I hit SEND and stretch out again, the sun beating down on me. Maybe it'll warm my skin enough so that when people touch me, they won't think I'm freezing. Still, I wonder if I should put on more sunblock. I slathered on a little SPF 15 back at the house. *In a minute*, I think, digging my toes into the sand. *I'll just rest and —*

"Excuse me?"

A boy's voice breaks into my dreamy thoughts.

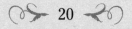

Annoyed, I blink a few times. A boy about my age is standing by my towel, wearing board shorts, a baseball cap, and a T-shirt that says S.M.A. BEARS. He's kind of cute, with curly brown hair, caramel-colored skin, and big brown eyes. I'm surprised I didn't hear him approach, but maybe, happily, my vampire-hearing isn't so sharp anymore.

"Yes?" I ask, sitting up and smiling. Wouldn't Eve and Mallory *really* be jealous if they knew I'd already found a possible crush?

"Well," the boy says shyly, shuffling his feet. "I don't mean to bother you, but, um . . . it looks like you've got a really bad burn."

"What are you talking about?" I snap, annoyed again. I glance down at my arms. They do look sort of red, but that's because I've got on my pink-tinted sunglasses.

I bristle. Who does this boy think he is? In New York, people know better than to bug random strangers out of nowhere.

"Maybe you should go to the lifeguard station," the boy is saying, not noticing my glare. "They have some special ointment if you want —"

"No, I don't *want* anything," I interrupt. "Leave me alone." This boy has *no* idea who he's messing with.

His face falls and he shrugs. "Okay, okay," he says, taking a few steps back. "Sorry about that."

"You'd better be," I mutter, watching him walk off down the beach. In a huff, I reach for my tote bag, ready to move to a different spot. But as soon as my hands make contact with the bag's handle, an intense pain shoots up from my palms.

"Ouch!" I cry. Confused, I whip off my sunglasses and stare down in horror at my hands, which are bright red. As are my arms . . . my gaze travels down . . . and my legs . . . my heart is thudding. I jump to my feet, which look like twin lobsters.

The boy was right. I have an awful sunburn. But how? I haven't been out here that long! I wonder if other people are noticing how burned-to-a-crisp I am. Panicked, I glance around. I have to get back to the house immediately.

I grab my tote bag and towel — *ouch!* — shove on my flip-flops, and start running across the sand. Suddenly, I'm dying for a Sanga!. I snuck one in New York this morning, but I shouldn't have gone this long without another. My throat is dry and my stomach is growling and I really, really hope I won't start to bat-shift. I feel like I'm about to collapse as I ring the bell to my new house.

When my mother opens the door, *she* looks like she might pass out. Her face goes white and her eyes bug out of her head.

"What on *earth* have you done?" she demands, grabbing my arm — *ouch!* — and pulling me inside. "Come, see for yourself," she adds, all but dragging me into the first-floor bathroom. She turns me toward the mirror . . .

. . . and I scream.

It's so much worse than I thought. My entire face is the color of a cherry tomato. It looks like someone splashed red paint across my collarbone and shoulders. Even my *eyeballs* look sunburned.

And I have to start a new school like this.

At that thought, I scream again. Talk about a horror movie.

"What's going on?" Dylan asks, appearing outside the bathroom. "I heard a scream —" He pauses, then doubles over in a fit of hysterical laughter. "Ba-ha-ha-ha!" he howls. "Hey, Ash, I think you have something on your face. . . . No, I mean . . . How was it, chillin' on the surface of the sun?" He can barely catch his breath between his dumb jokes.

I'm so mad I'm shaking. I feel like I could cry, but I don't want to give my brother the satisfaction. Instead,

I grab a magazine from my tote bag — *ouch!* — and fling it at his head. Unfortunately, he ducks.

"Dylan, leave your sister alone," Mom barks. As he scoots away, still laughing, Mom turns to me, looking disappointed. "I don't understand, Ashlee," she says crisply. "Haven't I taught you about proper skin care?" She sounds furious, like I chose to become a human fire engine on purpose. "I'm just glad I negotiated to not have you or your brother appear on the show," she mutters to herself.

"Mom, I don't know how this happened!" I wail. But deep down, I have a sneaking suspicion. I may have read about it in a book or seen it in a movie, but yes, I am pretty sure that vampires are supposed to stay out of the sun.

Except it doesn't make sense — back home, I could go out on sunny days and be fine. True, I was bundled up in a scarf and coat, since I've only been a vampire since the end of October. My thoughts are swirling, but I know there's one person I can turn to.

"I'll be right back," I tell my mom frantically. "I have to, um, call Eve."

"Wait —" Mom says, then shakes her head. "Fine. I need to pick up the new car from the dealer anyway. I'll stop at the drugstore on the way back to see if I can find something to fix this."

"Thanks!" I say, darting around her and dashing up the stairs. I'm relieved that she'll be gone for a while.

In my room, I take out my cell phone — *ouch!* — but before I can send a text, I see I have one waiting for me. A reply.

Sweet! Send us pix of ur tan. We're having hot cocoa & ice-skating! Eve & Mal

I feel a stab of hurt. I can never send my friends a picture of my (not exactly tan) self. But most of all, it bothers me that they're together, having cozy fun without me.

Whatever. I have more important things to deal with. I tap out a simple message, wincing as my sore fingers hit the keys:

EMERGENCY!

One endless minute later, my phone buzzes with an incoming call.

"What's wrong?" Arabella asks, her voice taut with worry. "What did you see? How badly are they hurt? Were there other witnesses?"

"Arabella, I look like a monster and you never told me that I wasn't supposed to go sunbathing and

now I have to go to school —" I stop babbling as her words sink in. "Wait, *what* did you say?"

Arabella sucks in a breath. "What did *you* say? You told me there was an emergency! I thought you were calling about . . ." She drops her voice to a whisper. *"Dark Ones."*

"Oh." I'd somehow forgotten all about Arabella's haunting warning. "That. Well, yeah. No. I got a bad sunburn."

There's a moment of silence, and I suspect Arabella is taking her deep yoga breaths, which she sometimes does when she's angry.

Then she speaks, slowly and carefully. "Ashlee, I'm at the office on a Sunday. Fashion Week is right around the corner, and things are crazy. Now, don't tell me you went to the beach or wore a bikini or just slapped on some SPF 15 or something?"

Now it's my turn to be silent. "All three," I finally whisper.

"Ashlee!" I hear her rings knock as she slaps her hand on her desk. "You're a vampire now. Our skin is very, very sensitive to sunlight, unless we're in bat form. In colder climates, it's not a problem. But you have to promise me that you will wear SPF 75 if you go to the beach. And it's best to wear long sleeves and pants if you'll be outside for a while. Oh, and sun hats."

"Sun hats?" I feel like crying again.

"Yes," Arabella says. "You should know this, Ashlee. It's in the Handbook."

Right. Arabella gave me the Transylvanian Vampire's Handbook back in November. I skimmed it, but it was totally boring. Right now, it's packed alongside my Sanga! cooler in my giant purple suitcase — the one Mom thought was suspiciously heavy this morning.

"Anyway, I need to go," Arabella is saying. "But remember, sweetie: SPF 75. Read the Handbook. And call me if you see anything —"

"Suspicious. I know, I know." I sigh, then tell Arabella good-bye and hang up.

My stomach growls as I walk over to the suit-cases that Mom must have brought up while I was out. I open my purple one — *ouch!* — and take out my Sanga! cooler. Once I'm finally sipping the sweet drink, I sink down onto the floor and rest my back against the wall. So much for my not being a vampire in LA.

I glance inside the suitcase, ignoring the black leather cover of the Handbook. My eyes drift mournfully over some of my wonderful warm-weather outfits. The blue-and-white romper; the yellow dress with the green trim; the lavender tank top . . . All fabulous options for my first day at Santa Monica Academy.

But not anymore.

Reluctantly, I pick up my phone and call my mother. She answers on the first ring.

"Hi, Mom," I say, forcing the words out. "Are you at the drugstore yet? I think I'm going to need a sun hat. . . ."

Chapter Three

Bright and early the next morning, Dylan and I are standing in front of Santa Monica Academy.

I'm wearing a long-sleeved gray T-shirt, jeans, sneakers, and sunglasses. The dreaded floppy blue sun hat Mom brought home yesterday covers my blond hair. To hide the redness on my face, I put on white pressed powder, which I fear has made me look like, well, a vampire.

This is *so* not how I imagined starting over in California.

"Let's go inside!" Dylan says excitedly. Kids are streaming past us and into the school, laughing and talking as the sunlight pours down on them. I realize that they all know one another already, and butterflies fill my belly.

"The same rules apply here," I mutter to my brother, and he nods as we walk toward the shiny glass doors.

Back in New York, our school was grades K through 12, which meant that Dylan and I were always in the same building (only in different sections). Santa Monica Academy is set up the same way. Fortunately, I came up with a set of rules years ago: Dylan and I ignore each other in the halls, and when asked if we're related, deny it.

Inside, we wordlessly part ways: Dylan heads left to the high school section, and I head right to the middle school. I sidestep a cluster of little kids trooping upstairs to the elementary section. Then I unzip my big patent-leather satchel, my hand brushing against my Sanga! mini-cooler. I remove the printout of my class schedule and confirm that first period is homeroom with Mr. Harker, in Room 105.

I make my way past a bunch of guys hanging up orange pennants that read GO BEARS! My heightened vision allows me to easily make out the numbers on the doors: 103 . . . 104 . . . 105. Fighting down a fresh wave of nerves, I enter the big, airy classroom.

The bell hasn't rung yet, so kids are still standing around and chatting. There are the Goth girls, all dressed in black with torn tights and sullen expressions. There are the geeky boys, crowding around someone's laptop (Dylan would fit in with them). There are the jocks, wearing gym shorts and the school colors, orange and gold.

Then I zero in on *my* kind.

In the center of the classroom stand three girls. One has a copper-colored ponytail and bronzed skin. She's wearing a white dress cinched with a yellow belt and matching yellow flats. The second girl is petite, with straight black hair. She wears denim shorts paired with boots — very LA. And the girl who's speaking, holding the attention of the other two, looks like a Barbie come to life. Blond ringlets fall to her shoulders and her lips are glossy. She has on a pink T-shirt, a floral-print skirt, and the same wedge espadrilles that *I own*.

The way the blond girl holds herself — one hand on her hip, smiling coolly at her friends — reminds me of someone. Then I realize: She reminds me . . . of myself. This girl is the Ashlee Lambert of Santa Monica Academy.

Or, at least, the Ashlee I used to be, before bats starting showing up at my bedroom window.

But somehow, seeing this girl fills me with

confidence. What was I so nervous about? I'm still *me*. And I'm still going to start fresh. Starting now.

I lift my chin, take off my sunglasses, and march toward the popular girls. Some of the Goths and jocks look at me, shocked. Clearly, other new kids usually aren't so brave.

I come to a stop in front of the blond girl. She pauses mid-sentence and raises an eyebrow at me.

"Hi," I say. "I'm Ashlee Lambert. I just moved here from New York City."

The blond girl purses her lips. The two others watch her, waiting. I feel my palms start to sweat.

"Hi there, Ashlee," the blond says at last, her voice almost too sugary sweet. "I'm Paige Olsen. Introduce yourselves, girls," she adds, keeping her eyes on me.

"I'm Wendy Lee," says the black-haired girl, giving me a tiny, hesitant smile.

"Carmen Espinoza," says the girl with the pony-tail, her voice curt.

"Nice to meet you," I say, looking right at Paige.

My heart lifts with hope. This is it. These girls will welcome me into their fold, make me the fourth member of their crew. I picture all of us going shopping in Beverly Hills. Hanging out in one another's bedrooms. Getting mani-pedis. Maybe Eve and

Mallory will fly out to visit me, and the six of us will all have fun together.

And soon enough, I'll nudge Paige out of the way. *I'll* be the one that the other girls pay closest attention to, and that every kid in the school will know.

"So tell us, Ashlee," Paige says slowly, tapping one espadrille against the floor. I wish desperately that I'd worn *my* espadrilles today, but my feet were too sore and red. As if she knows what I'm thinking, Paige's eyes travel from my bulky sneakers up to my face. "Are you in . . . *disguise*?" she asks.

Wendy and Carmen titter, and my stomach sinks.

"Yeah," Carmen jumps in. "Are you, like, a spy or something?"

"Or maybe she's cold," Wendy coos.

Flustered, I yank off my sun hat. How did I forget to remove it? I shake out my hair, hoping the girls will notice its lustrous quality and realize that *I'm one of them*. And I'm not dressed *that* atrociously. I even have a designer bag! I try to hold it up in a subtle way.

But I can tell it's too late. The girls are exchanging knowing glances and rolling their eyes. *At me.* A lump forms in my throat. This isn't supposed to be happening!

I open my mouth to explain about my sunburn — although, would that make me sound even dorkier? — but then the bell rings. Kids start to take their seats.

"Later, *Rash*-lee," Paige drawls, leading Carmen and Wendy away. The girls burst into giggles, and I hear Carmen murmur, "Did you see how her hands were all red?"

Hot tears blur my vision and I drop into the first available seat. *Why do I have to be a vampire?* I think, anger growing in my chest. *It's ruining everything!*

"Ignore them," a voice says beside me.

I swipe at my eyes and glance to my left. The girl sitting there has curly light brown hair, wide hazel eyes, and skin the color of a latte. She's pretty, but she's wearing a purple T-shirt and a necklace of big orange beads. Neon blue bangles slide up and down her arms. Everything clashes. There's no way she's in the popular crowd.

"Those girls," she continues. "They love to be mean every chance they get. But you can't take them seriously."

I squirm in my seat. I hate that this weirdly dressed girl overheard how Paige insulted me. I hate that she's taking pity on me. I wish she'd mind her own business.

"I'm fine," I tell her shortly, then face forward as the teacher walks in.

"Good morning, everyone!" booms Mr. Harker, who is surprisingly young and handsome — for a teacher. He has sandy hair and cool, black-framed glasses. "I trust you all had a nice winter break?"

"I went to Hawaii!" Paige bubbles from her seat.

"And no one cares," the girl next to me says under her breath. For some reason this almost makes me laugh, but then I decide it's not funny.

"Well," says Mr. Harker, blowing his nose with a tissue, "I was laid up with the flu, so I was not so lucky. Ah," he adds, lifting up a piece of paper from his desk. "I see we have a new student in our midst. Ashlee Lambert, can you please make your presence known?"

I raise my hand and hear snickers coming from Paige's area. My stomach turns.

"Welcome, Ms. Lambert," Mr. Harker says. "I'll also be your sixth period English teacher. Please let me know if you have any questions."

I do, I think. *I'd like to know if there's any way for me to become popular.* But I keep quiet, folding my sunburned hands and looking down as Mr. Harker takes attendance. I learn that the girl next to me is named Sasha Hirsh, which sounds familiar, but I can't figure out why.

"All right," says Mr. Harker when he's done. "I want to remind folks that we still need a wardrobe master for the seventh-grade play. Opening night's in less than two weeks! I'm the director, so come speak to me if you want to sign up for the position."

"And I'm the star," Paige announces haughtily, turning in her seat. "We had to fire our last wardrobe master because she had a *terrible* sense of style." She shudders, and Carmen and Wendy nod emphatically.

I perk up. Now that I can't ever be in movies or on TV, the theater is a great new option. It's obvious that Paige and her friends are very involved in the play. If I become a part of it, too, that will give me a shot at joining their group! And though I'd rather be onstage, wardrobe master does sound right up my alley.

"Which play is it?" I ask. Paige narrows her eyes at me.

"It's called *At First Bite*," Sasha answers, her bracelets clanking as she turns to me. "I'm the stage manager," she explains.

I frown. Haven't I heard that title before?

"It's based on a classic vampire movie that was filmed right here in Santa Monica," Mr. Harker says. "You probably haven't seen it, Ashlee, but I showed it to the cast and crew when we started rehearsals back in November. It's really thrilling."

That's when it hits me. "*At First Bite* was filmed at my house!" I blurt out. A chill shoots through me. I had no idea the movie was about vampires — though I guess the title should have been a giveaway.

"Really?" Mr. Harker asks, raising his eyebrows. "What a funny coincidence."

A creepy coincidence, I think. I shiver in the warm classroom.

"Rash-lee lives in a horror-movie house?" I hear Paige giggle from across the room. "That explains a lot!"

Wendy, Carmen, and a few other kids join in the laughter. For a terrifying second, I think that they *know* — they've figured out my secret. But as the laughter builds, I understand that no, they just think I'm a freak.

Rage and embarrassment bubble inside me. I clench my hands into fists and bend my head forward, letting my hair curtain my face. Thanks to my heightened hearing, each classmate's laugh sounds like a small explosion. This is my worst nightmare. This is even worse than turning into a bat unexpectedly.

And speaking of which —

I feel the fangs first, starting at the corners of my mouth. Slowly, they push forward, sharp and pointy, over my lips.

Oh no.

Next my face begins to shrink, my skin tightening across my cheekbones and my nose taking on a snoutlike shape.

It's happening. I'm transforming. Here, in my new school. My heart bangs against my ribs and I jump up so fast I almost knock over my desk. It's not a question of if I should leave the room but how quickly.

Keeping my head down, I sprint toward the door.

"Ashlee, hold on!" Mr. Harker calls. He blocks my path, and I glance up. My eyes must have already turned bloodred; I can tell from the way they burn. Mr. Harker's own eyes widen for a heartbeat, but I move too fast for him to see any more. I keep running, my feet curling into claws inside my sneakers.

"Silence, class," I hear Mr. Harker snap as I stumble out into the hallway. "Is that any way to welcome a new student? You should be ashamed of yourselves."

Fine. Whatever. Let Mr. Harker, let everyone think that I ran out of there in tears. Right now every piece of me is focused on getting to a private spot as fast as is humanly — or bat-ly — possible.

I'm relieved to find the halls empty: Everyone is tucked inside classrooms, at least until the bell rings. So no one can see my arms bending inward and becoming webbed, leathery wings. No one can see my body shrink upward. I'm racked with panic. *I need to find a bathroom.* I feel my ears stretching to the top of my head. *A bathroom. Now.*

Up ahead, I spot a silver-haired man in a janitor's uniform pushing a mop across the floor. Thankfully, he doesn't look up, and as he moves aside, I see it: a girls' bathroom.

In that same moment, the bell rings. I hold my breath and throw my body against the bathroom door, flying inside.

Yes, literally flying.

Because by now, I'm a bat.

I catch a horrific glimpse of myself in the bath-room mirror: a small winged creature, hovering in midair. My eyes are beady and red, and my fangs glint under the fluorescent lights. This is who I am now.

Voices and footsteps fill the hallway outside, and I hear a girl say, "I need to reapply my mascara before class. Come with?"

Frantic, I zip into one of the stalls. The *whoosh* of my wings forces the stall door to close behind me. I wedge myself into a corner. As my claws dig into the cold tiles, my bat body automatically flips upside down. I feel dizzy, but this is the only way for me to stay perched here. So I fold my wings tight against myself and wait.

The mascara girl and her friend clatter into the bathroom, talking about winter break. I hope that Paige and her crew won't decide to stop in here. It would be just my luck for, say, Carmen to discover me and try to smack me with her book bag. Arabella has told me plenty of stories about being chased by screaming people shaking broomsticks. And she's an experienced shifter.

I try to imagine what Arabella would say if she were here. She'd probably tell me to calm down, since getting worked up is usually what causes me to shift in the first place. I take a few deep breaths and wish I'd read the Vampire's Handbook last night instead of the latest issue of *Us Weekly*.

"So did you hear about the cute new guy in the high school?" the mascara girl says. I have nothing better to do right now, so I listen in.

"The sophomore?" her friend says, turning off the sink. "Yeah, Dylan something? I saw him standing outside earlier, I think."

Wait. Dylan something?

No. It can't be.

"Blond hair, blue eyes, totally gorg?" the other girl asks, zipping up her makeup case. "I heard he's from New York City."

My claws slip and I almost fall into the open toilet. There's *no way* these girls could be talking about *my brother*. My socially awkward, doofy brother, who, back home, couldn't get a girl to look at him if he walked into her.

But how many blond, blue-eyed, sophomore Dylans from New York City can there be?

"Do you think a sophomore would ever date an eighth grader?" the mascara girl asks as they head for the door.

"A guy like *that*? Dream on." The door slams behind them.

If bats could roll their eyes, I would. *Totally gorg?* Dylan? It makes no sense! He's being drooled over by girls, and I'm being shunned by the popular crowd. Has the world gone mad?

I'm so distracted, I don't even notice that I'm starting to shift back. My fangs are receding into my mouth, becoming regular teeth. My ears slide down to their normal spot as my legs stretch out. When vampires bat-shift, our clothes dissolve but reappear as soon as we shift back. I'm relieved to see my jeans pop back into place and my shirt fabric spread across my arms.

The only problem is, I'm still upside down, and my clingy claws are becoming human feet again. How am I going to manage this? My pulse races as I try to clamber into an upright position. I reach for the stall door with one hand, but I'm feeling very clumsy, and suddenly the bell is ringing, shrill and close to my ear. Then I lose my grip entirely. My stomach drops, and I plummet toward the floor.

At least I missed the toilet, I think as my forehead smacks against the linoleum.

And then everything goes black.

Chapter Four

I open my eyes to weak sunlight coming in through drawn shades. I'm in a small white room that smells like rubbing alcohol, and I'm lying on something soft — a cot, my hazy brain registers. A poster on the wall shows a cat clinging to a tree branch with the words HANG IN THERE, BABY! printed underneath. Considering what I've just been through, this seems especially cruel.

I try to sit up, but a pudgy woman in light blue scrubs immediately rushes over.

"Take it easy, honey," she tells me, taking my shoulders and guiding me back down onto the scratchy pillow.

"Am I in the hospital?" I ask in a raspy voice.

The woman smiles, shaking her head. "Just the

nurse's office. I'm Nurse Murray. You took a nasty spill. Remember?"

"I remember," I groan. A throbbing pain is shooting across my forehead. I reach up and feel the giant welt that's forming there. Great. My first day of school keeps getting better and better.

"It's only a bump. No concussion," Nurse Murray assures me. "But let me get you a fresh ice pack." She hurries off to the refrigerator in the corner.

I prop myself up on one elbow and gaze around the room. There are two other (empty) cots, a desk, and a first-aid kit on the wall. Then I notice my patent-leather satchel on a chair, along with my sun hat and sunglasses.

"Who brought my stuff in?" I ask. I'd left everything in homeroom, hadn't I? My head swims. Now that I think about it, I do have a fuzzy memory of someone helping me up off the bathroom floor and then walking with me down a flight of stairs. I vaguely recall stretching out on this cot and falling asleep. But that's all.

"Your friend," the nurse answers, returning with the ice pack. "She was so sweet, helping you down here and making sure you were okay."

"My friend?" I repeat, now really confused. I'm not sure how to break this to kindhearted Nurse Murray, but I don't *have* any friends at the moment.

"I'm afraid I don't know her name," Nurse Murray says, pressing the ice pack to my forehead. "I'm new to the school, you see. But she had curly brown hair and was wearing bright colors: a purple shirt and a big orange necklace."

That could only be Sasha, the unpopular girl from homeroom. I frown. Had she followed me to the bathroom? Why? And — my heart jumps — what condition had she found me in? Had I finished shifting all the way back?

"What did — what did she say?" I stammer, jerking away so that the ice pack falls into my lap.

"Just that you slipped in the girls' room," Nurse Murray replies, looking at me with a suspicious expression. "That *is* what happened, right?"

"Um . . . yeah," I reply, my palms growing clammy. Did I tell Sasha that? What else went on that I can't remember?

Suddenly, I worry that Nurse Murray took my temperature or drew blood from me. Or if she hasn't, maybe she plans to. Vampires have a lower body temperature than most people: It's why our skin is cold to the touch. And our blood is a very deep crimson color, almost black. Arabella told me that some doctors don't find these details strange, but others do.

I realize I need to leave before Nurse Murray notices how strange I am.

"You know, I'm actually feeling much better," I say, swinging my legs off the cot. It's true, too; though the welt on my forehead hurts, I'm not dizzy. "I should get to second period," I add, slowly standing up. "I think I have math —"

"Second period?" Nurse Murray checks her watch and chuckles. "Forget it, honey! It's fourth period. Lunchtime for you middle schoolers."

"I slept that long?" I ask, startled. I guess after the trauma of homeroom, bat-shifting, and my accident, I needed the rest.

Nurse Murray nods. "I really shouldn't let you go yet," she says worriedly. "I was thinking of calling your parents to see if they wanted to take you home for the day."

I'm torn. Part of me wants to get far away from Santa Monica Academy and hide in my bedroom. But another piece of me wants to stay and fight my way into Paige's crowd. To prove to everyone that they were wrong about me this morning.

"My mom isn't around," I tell Nurse Murray truthfully. "She's being filmed all day and won't be home until later."

Nurse Murray's eyes light up. "Is your mom . . . a celebrity?" she asks in a hushed, awed tone.

"Kind of." I'd never thought of my mom that way, but I'm sure *she'd* love to hear it. "She's a judge, and they're making a reality show about her."

"You mean *Justice with Judge Julia*?" Nurse Murray gasps, and claps her hands when I nod. "There was a piece on it in *Variety*, you know, the newspaper about Hollywood deals? I love to read that paper and imagine all the producers and stars doing exciting things." The nurse looks starry-eyed.

A lightbulb goes off in my head. "Well, I'm sure I could get you my mom's autograph. . . ." I stare meaningfully at Nurse Murray. *If you let me go now*, I add silently.

Nurse Murray seems to get my message. "That would be wonderful," she says, looking a little embarrassed but still beaming. She bustles over to her desk and writes me a pass for the classes I missed.

I gather my belongings and am almost to the door when she speaks up behind me.

"One last thing, dear?"

I turn around, scared that she'll ask me more about my accident.

"Take care of that sunburn, will you?" she says. "It's dreadful."

"Tell me about it," I sigh.

I don't know the way to the cafeteria. But, as usual, I can smell the food from afar, so I follow the scent. *Spaghetti and meatballs*, I think hungrily as I reach the double doors. When I get in the lunch line, I see the meal is actually whole-wheat penne with organic lamb meatballs. There's also a juice station and an organic salad bar. How California!

Once my recycled-aluminum tray is piled high, I scan the crowded lunchroom. My heart races. Kids are waving to one another, taking seats and sipping carrot-and-ginger smoothies. I don't recognize any-one, and my sneakers seem glued to the floor. I never thought I'd be *that* kind of new kid, the one without a place to sit in the cafeteria.

"Ashlee?"

Excited, I spin around and see Sasha, sitting alone at a round table.

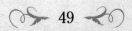

Ugh. My spirits fall. Is this girl stalking me or something?

"Are you okay?" Sasha asks, looking concerned. "I took you to the nurse's —"

"I know, I know," I hiss, not wanting the whole world to hear about my mishap. I move closer to Sasha, awkwardly balancing my heavy tray. "Yeah, um, how did you find me? And what was I —"

"Do you want to sit?" Sasha cuts in, gesturing to my wobbling tray with a small smile on her face. "Might be easier to talk that way."

I hesitate, glancing around. I can't spot Paige, Wendy, or Carmen. But sitting with *someone* beats sitting alone, even if that someone is Sasha. And I suppose I should be grateful to her and all.

"Fine," I say stiffly, dropping down into a chair. "Just for a minute."

"Got it," Sasha says, still smiling.

"Anyway," I say, not meeting her gaze. "Thanks . . . for what you did."

"No problem," Sasha replies, spearing an avocado slice in her salad. "When you ran out of homeroom, I was worried —"

"Would you keep it down?" I hiss, glancing around again. Sasha's voice is as loud as her clothes.

"Sorry," Sasha replies in an exaggerated whisper, and I roll my eyes. "I was worried," she continues quietly, "so when the bell rang, I took your stuff and went to the bathroom down the hall."

"How did you know I'd be there?" I ask around a mouthful of pasta.

Sasha shrugs. "Just a guess. It's the same bathroom I used to cry in when Paige and her cronies made fun of me."

I reel back. Now I know for sure how unpopular Sasha is. But . . .

"What do you mean, 'used to'?" I ask. Did Paige not make fun of Sasha anymore?

Sasha calmly sips her juice. "I let it stop bothering me," she says matter-of-factly. "I realized that there was more to life than getting the approval of those girls, and as soon as I came to that conclusion, they no longer had an effect on me."

I stare at Sasha blankly. I have no clue what she's talking about.

"So," she goes on, taking a bite of penne, "I got to the bathroom and saw your feet sticking out from one of the stalls. I realized you must have slipped. The janitor, Mr. Bernal, is so nice, but he's always mopping the bathrooms first thing in the morning."

"And . . . how did I look?" I ask carefully, petrified that Sasha will say that she saw me with bat ears.

She shakes her head and laughs. "Is that always your main concern?" she asks, and I scowl at her. "You looked, I don't know, out of it. Your eyes were all big and you kept muttering something about your brother."

"Oh yeah," I mutter now, remembering the eighth-grade girls gushing over Dylan. Yet another reason to hate my brother. My fall was *so* his fault.

"Does your brother go to this school?" Sasha asks, and I nod reluctantly. "Mine does, too — oh, there he is now!" she exclaims, waving to someone across the room. "Hey, Marc," she says a moment later as a boy sets his tray down at the table. "I was wondering where you were."

"I had some stuff to do," the boy answers. His voice sounds familiar.

I look up at him and freeze.

Marc has curly brown hair and big brown eyes. Marc is the boy who bugged me about my sunburn on the beach!

He's staring back at me in surprise, so I know he recognizes me, too. I hold my breath, hoping he won't say anything. Especially something like *I told you so.* My sunburn seems to grow hotter and I'm sure my cheeks are even redder than before.

"Marc, this is Ashlee Lambert. Ashlee, meet Marc Hirsh," Sasha says.

Marc is still looking at me. I can tell he's wondering whether or not to say that we've already met. I squirm in my seat, hoping he'll keep quiet.

Finally, Sasha smacks his arm. "You'll have to excuse my twin," she tells me. "He doesn't know how to talk to humans. Just computers."

"Thanks, sis," Marc says, plopping down beside her. He shoots me a quick half smile before digging into his pasta. I let out a breath. I'm pretty sure that, for now, our encounter on the beach will stay secret.

I study Marc and Sasha. I wouldn't have pegged them for twins, but there is a definite resemblance. Marc is wearing a T-shirt that says ARCADE FIRE, and I remember that his shirt yesterday said S.M.A. BEARS. Of course. Santa Monica Academy Bears: I've seen the football pennants everywhere today. Though Marc doesn't strike me as a jock. I'm wondering what group he belongs to when another boy runs up to our table.

"What's up, dudes?" he asks, slapping Marc and Sasha high fives. He has reddish hair and big glasses.

I immediately recognize him as one of the geeky boys from homeroom. True to form, he plunks himself down next to Marc and opens his laptop. "I just came from the computer lab," he says as Marc leans over to look at the screen. "I found a way to add bandwidth to the —"

"Gordon, you remember Ashlee from homeroom, right?" Sasha cuts in. I'm glad she doesn't mention that I'm the girl everyone laughed at.

Baffled, Gordon glances up and nods at me distractedly. Then he turns his attention back to his laptop, where Marc is now typing something in.

Well, that answers that. Marc is part of the geeky group. Which means, by extension, Sasha is, too. And since *I'm sitting with them* . . .

Ack!

I push my chair back, full of anxiety. I can't be seen with these people: It could ruin me forever! I scan the lunchroom again. This time, I do spot Paige, Carmen, and Wendy. They're sitting at a prime table by the window, surrounded by cute guys in polo shirts and some other girls in cheerleader uniforms. The popular table. A wave of longing washes over me.

All I want to do is dash over and join them, but I realize that wouldn't be the wisest move. Paige would probably mock the welt on my forehead. No. I need to come up with a plan, a natural way to ease myself into the group.

"Guys," Sasha is saying, "stop working on that social networking website. You have to focus on the music cues for the play. You know Paige is going to bite your head off at rehearsals if the sound isn't perfect."

I swivel my head back to Sasha. *The play!* I'd forgotten about it. That was going to be my chance to get in good with Paige and her friends. I feel a flush of relief. Perfect.

"You're the stage manager, right?" I ask Sasha, who nods proudly.

"And we're the tech crew," Marc pipes up, gesturing to himself and Gordon. "Sound and lighting. We make sure that the music plays at the right times and that the actors don't look too . . . pink or anything." He grins at me and I glare at him.

Sasha looks at us quizzically, but Marc turns his attention back to the laptop. "You asked about the play in homeroom," Sasha says to me. "Are you interested in the wardrobe master position?"

I bite my lip, hesitating. I don't love that the stage crew is full of unpopular kids . . . *or* that the play itself is about vampires. But I can't let that stop me. Too much is riding on this.

"I am," I say. "I love fashion. I think I'd be the right fit."

"Cool. You need to check with Mr. Harker," Sasha says, looking around the cafeteria. "He's usually one of the lunchroom monitors, but I don't see him. You can e-mail him about it. Teachers are really into e-mail here."

She smiles at me, as if we're friends now. *Yeah, right.*

I glance back at the popular table. Paige is giggling at something one of the boys is saying. Then she happens to look in my direction. Her eyes sweep over my tablemates, and she smirks. My stomach clenches. This is what I'd feared.

"I'm off," I tell Sasha and the guys abruptly, standing up. I grab my bag and tray.

"Did the bell ring?" Gordon asks, looking up from his laptop dazedly.

"No," I say coolly. "I have something important to do."

What I need to do — besides escape from the Table of Social Doom — is hustle over to a quiet space and suck down a Sanga! I know that if I wait too long, I'll be shaky later on. I don't really want to pass out in fifth period history and have to pay another visit to Nurse Murray's office.

"I'm sure you do," Sasha says, sounding amused. Does she think she's better than me or something? I'm about to snap at her when my tray starts to slide out of my grip. I extend my arms to catch it, and my satchel falls, landing at Marc's feet.

"I'll get it," he says, bending over. Horrified, I realize that the bag is half unzipped and he might see my Sanga! mini-cooler. Not that he'd know what it was. Still, I slam my tray on the table and dive forward.

"Give — it — to me," I say through gritted teeth, yanking on the bag's handle. Marc looks at me like I'm crazy. I yank harder and win the tug-of-war. Then I turn and head for the cafeteria doors without glancing back.

As soon as I'm outside, I breathe easier. I look up and down the empty hall, wondering where to seek shelter and drink my Sanga! Maybe the library?

But before I can move, I hear a bloodcurdling scream rip through the school.

Chapter Five

I don't think, I just run, right toward where the scream came from. I round a corner and see a small crowd gathered in front of the janitor's closet. Two young-looking girls — probably sixth graders — are sobbing, and a few teachers are murmuring together.

Then I see Nurse Murray. It's clear she was the one who screamed. Her mouth is open in an *O* of shock, and her face is ghost white. She is pointing to the floor, where the silver-haired janitor I'd seen earlier is lying.

His legs are inside the closet, among the mops and brooms and cleaning supplies. He's staring up at the ceiling, his eyes as wide as dinner plates. He's alive; I can see his chest rising and falling with breath. But there's a terrible wound on his neck: Two bloody punctures, like those made by fangs.

My stomach lurches, and I reach out to grab the arm of the girl standing nearest to me.

"What happened?" I ask her, my voice coming out strangled.

"We don't know," she whimpers. "Someone tried to hurt Mr. Bernal!"

"I — I found him," Nurse Murray finally croaks out. By now a larger crowd has gathered, and her eyes dart from person to person. "I was having tomato soup for lunch and I spilled it all over my desk. I came to the janitor's closet for some sponges, and when I opened the door, he — he fell out! All frozen like this."

Cries ripple through the crowd, and the two sobbing girls hug each other. I can't tear my eyes away from Mr. Bernal's wound. It looks . . . familiar.

I remember the night I became full-fledged, when I had to follow the older vampires on a hunt through Central Park. By the light of the full moon, I watched them swoop down on little birds and squirrels, leaving the animals with the same kind of puncture marks in their necks. Unlike Mr. Bernal, the small animals didn't survive. The vampires had drained their blood.

Now my own blood runs cold. Mr. Bernal's attack can't possibly mean what I'm thinking. Can it?

"Excuse me, coming through!" calls an imposing voice, and I turn to see a tall, gray-haired woman parting the crowd. I recognize her from the school website: It's the principal, Ms. Anderson. A few more teachers, including Mr. Harker, trail behind her.

"What's going on here? Do we need to call an ambulance?" Ms. Anderson demands. "You're the new nurse, aren't you?" she asks Nurse Murray in a bossy tone.

Nurse Murray blinks, as if remembering that she is, in fact, a medical professional. She kneels beside the janitor and puts her fingers to his wrist, taking his pulse. Then she gently taps his shoulder and says, "Sir? Sir? Can you talk to us?"

We all hold our breath as Mr. Bernal slowly lifts his head.

"There was a b —, a b —" he stammers, raspy-voiced. His face is ashen and he seems too weak to say more. Nurse Murray pats his arm in an encouraging way. Closing his eyes, the janitor forces the word out. "Bat," he says. "There was a bat."

My knees buckle, and the hallway spins. There are more murmurs around me, but this time they sound hollow and distant. *A bat.*

"It came flying right at me as I was stepping out of the closet," Mr. Bernal continues, sitting up and looking frantic. "I felt it latch on to my neck and I fell backward. . . . That's the last thing I remember." He puts his hand to his throat and then stares in horror at the blood on his fingers.

"Ew! There are bats in the school?" someone shrieks. I glance over my shoulder and see that it's Paige, flanked by Wendy, Carmen, and others from the popular table.

"Yeah, can we call an exterminator?" Wendy demands.

"Exterminators are for bugs, not flying mammals," Sasha snaps. She's standing on the fringes of the crowd with Marc and Gordon.

"A bat?" Nurse Murray asks Mr. Bernal, sounding doubtful. She takes a pen flashlight from the pocket of her scrubs and shines it into his eyes. "Are you sure you didn't just fall and cut your neck on a cleaning tool?" she offers.

Mr. Bernal shakes his head. "I know what I saw," he insists.

"Maybe we *should* call an ambulance," I hear Mr. Harker say to the principal. He spins a finger next to his head and mouths the words *nervous breakdown*. Principal Anderson nods, looking somber, and she whispers, "We've been on him to retire for years now."

They think that Mr. Bernal is crazy. They think he imagined the bat entirely.

But I know better.

"Okay, everyone, show's over! Break it up and get to class," Ms. Anderson shouts, clapping her hands.

On cue, the bell rings and people scurry in all directions, still buzzing over the incident. I should hurry to history, but I remain rooted to the spot, my thoughts churning.

I'm certain that Mr. Bernal was attacked by a vampire. Arabella said there are Dark Ones — vampires who feast on human blood — here in Los Angeles. True, this vampire could have snuck into the building. But what if he or she came from inside the school?

I study the thinning crowd. Is there another vampire at Santa Monica Academy besides me? A Dark One, no less?

Suddenly, my sharp vision catches something I hadn't seen before: a tiny spot of red near Nurse

Murray's mouth. Sweet, caring Nurse Murray? I watch her carefully as she helps Mr. Bernal to his feet. She'd said she'd had tomato soup for lunch, but she could have been lying. She was the one to find the janitor, after all. And she's new to the school: People don't know much about her.

But when I was in her office earlier, she'd seemed perfectly normal. If anything, I was the one acting weird.

And then I think of something that chills me to the bone.

After I fell in the bathroom, there was a period of time that I can't quite recall. For all I know, I could have shifted back to bat form. *I could have flown over to the janitor's closet and attacked Mr. Bernal.*

What if I'm a Dark One and I don't even know it?

"You are so not a Dark One," Arabella tells me on the phone that evening. "Would you relax?"

"But how are you so sure?" I ask, flopping down on my air mattress. I can't wait for my real furniture to arrive.

After Mr. Bernal's attack, the rest of the day had passed uneventfully. Classes at S.M.A. were similar to classes back in New York, except that gym was devoted to yoga, and science had a special unit on the dangers of plastic surgery. Sasha was in my math class, Marc was in history, and Paige was in English, but I didn't interact with anyone. The fact that I'd made it through the afternoon with no new injuries felt like a victory.

"Trust me," Arabella replies, typing as she talks. New York is three hours ahead of LA, but Arabella is often at her office late at night. "Dark Ones tend to get sick if they go too long without human blood, and you haven't had so much as a sniffle since I met you. Plus, you're a softy inside, Ashlee. You wouldn't set out to harm anyone."

"I'm not a softy!" I argue, applying aloe gel to my neon pink arms. "In New York, my friends always did what I said."

It's true. Eve and Mallory used to follow my lead, no questions asked. I sigh, remembering the good old days.

Arabella snorts. "Those sound like healthy friendships," she says sarcastically, and I frown. "Anyway, it's good you called me with this update. I'll e-mail the Los Angeles Council and tell them to be on alert for any more signs of Dark Ones."

In every city there is a Council made up of older, important vampires who meet regularly to discuss — well, I'm not sure. Vampire matters, I suppose. Like the decision to make Sanga! accessible worldwide. It might be kind of cool to be on the Council someday.

"Okay," I say, setting down the tube of aloe gel. "I'll keep you posted, too."

"Oh, hang on," Arabella tells me. I hear her shout to someone else, "There are no seats at the Dolce and Gabbana show?" She groans. "Ash? I'm sorry, but I need to —"

"I know, Fashion Week," I grumble. For the first time ever, I kind of resent fashion. "Listen," I add quickly. "What can I do to avoid bat-shifting out of nowhere?" I massage the welt on my forehead.

"You'll get the hang of it, I promise," Arabella says. "Stay calm, read the Handbook, and practice. I'll call soon." And with a click, she's gone.

Still feeling rattled, I walk over to my desk. I'm too jittery to read the Handbook or do homework, so I check my e-mail. I wrote to Eve and Mallory as soon as I got home from school, filling them in on my *amazing* day. I made no mention of being socially scorned, or clonking my head, or seeing fang marks on the janitor. There's no need for them to know those details.

But neither of my friends has written back.

I open my door and peer out into the dark hall-way. Mom is having dinner with some people from the studio, and Dylan, believe it or not, is hanging out with friends. Yes, *friends.* Who actually sound like they could be cool. As we walked home from school, he told me that he'd met some guys in home-room who were Rock Band champions, and they'd invited him to go skateboarding. He'd been grinning like an idiot, and all I could think about were those eighth-grade girls in the bathroom, saying he was gorgeous. It had taken all my self-control not to sucker-punch my brother.

The empty house feels a little eerie tonight, and it makes me think of *At First Bite* being filmed here, years and years ago. I realize that if I want to be wardrobe master for the play, I need to know more about the actual story. So, grabbing a fresh Sanga!, I head downstairs to the living room TV. Luckily, Dylan took care of hooking up our Wii, so I can access our Netflix streaming account. I select the movie, then settle back on a folding chair to watch.

The movie is old, like black-and-white old, and it takes place in what is supposed to be 1789 Transylvania. But I can tell it's Los Angeles (they didn't do a very good job hiding the palm trees). The main character is a blond peasant girl named Vera who works as a maid for a wealthy, mysterious, dark-haired guy named Vladimir. His "castle" is, of course, our house. I even recognize my own bedroom (where Vera sleeps), which sends a shiver down my back. Vera keeps seeing and hearing strange things, like funny shadows on the walls and screams in the night. But at the same time she's also falling in love with the charming Vladimir.

It's obvious to anyone with half a brain that Vladimir is a vampire, and I smile at all the clichés. He sleeps during the day (in a bed that looks conveniently like a coffin) and trembles at the sight of garlic (true fact: I love garlic and always put a ton on my pizza). Spooky, over-the-top music plays whenever he appears, but love-struck Vera doesn't get the message. One night, she even sees a swarm of bats — clearly puppets pulled by strings — flying toward her. She dramatically faints, but when she comes to, she brushes off her lace apron and goes back to kneading dough.

Sipping my Sanga!, I shake my head. *Being* a vampire is a whole lot scarier than a movie about one could ever be. A movie can't capture the uncertainty I feel every day, wondering when my teeth might turn into fangs. A movie can't re-create the terror I felt that afternoon, seeing Mr. Bernal's neck wound and knowing what I was capable of.

Still, I find myself holding my breath when Vera finds Vladimir in the (our) living room, biting the neck of a prissy society girl named Mila. Vladimir whirls around to Vera, his fangs bared and bloody, as Mila drops dead. Understandably, Vera freaks out, but he tells her he loves her and wants to make her a vampire, too. Vera agrees, and he bites her neck just long enough to transform her (there's no initiation ceremony). The movie ends with them both as bats, flying off happily toward a crescent moon.

As the credits are rolling, I hear the front door creak open. I shriek, jumping to my feet and knocking over my empty cup of Sanga!

I guess I was more scared than I realized.

"It's just us," Mom laughs. She walks in with Dylan, who is still smiling in that self-satisfied way. "Your brother called me from his friend's house, so I gave him a lift home," she explains. "What were you watching?"

"Nothing," I answer, too quickly. I scoop up my cup, then hold it behind my back as I shut off the TV.

I glance around the living room, almost expecting to see Vladimir and Vera embracing, with Mila's bloodless corpse sprawled on the floor behind them. I can't believe it. Somehow the movie, with all its cheesiness and fakeness, actually had an effect on me, a real-life vampire! I bet non-vampires watching it would get even more sucked in. No wonder Mr. Harker said it was "really thrilling."

Mom waves Dylan and me upstairs, clucking about homework and bedtime. I return to my room, but my thoughts are elsewhere. I imagine Vera in here, wearing a silken dressing gown. Maybe in the play, her signature color can be green, so the gown should have green accents on the sleeves. My heart pounds with excitement and inspiration. For the first time that night, I'm not worrying about Dark Ones, or bat-shifting, or my sorry social status. I don't even check my e-mail to see if Eve or Mallory have written back.

Instead, I log in to my Santa Monica Academy e-mail account and compose what I hope is a professional-sounding message:

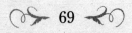

Dear Mr. Harker,

I'm not sure you remember me, but I'm a new seventh grader. If the position is still open, I would like to be wardrobe master for *At First Bite*. I just watched the movie, and I have lots of ideas!

Sincerely,
Ashlee Lambert

Nervously, I hit SEND, certain I won't hear from him until tomorrow. But as I'm about to log off, I get a response.

Dear Ashlee,

The position is indeed still open. I'm sure living in Vladimir's "castle" is doubly inspirational for you! Please come to our next rehearsal this Thursday after school in the auditorium. You can run your ideas by me, as well as the cast and crew.

Regards,
Mr. Harker

Yes! Grinning, I slap my laptop shut and crawl onto my air mattress, bone-tired but content. The long, hard day catches up with me, and my eyes close. As the ocean moans outside, I drift off, dreaming of espadrilles, tomato soup, and crescent moons.

Chapter Six

I spend the next two days on pins and needles.

I jot down costume ideas in my notebook, and observe Paige and her friends in the classes we share. Aside from murmurs of "*Rash*-lee," followed by snickers in my direction, the glowing group basically acts like I don't exist.

I, in turn, ignore Sasha, Marc, and Gordon, not wanting to be poisoned by their unpopularity. During lunch, I hide out in the library, where I can drink my Sanga! in private.

It's a lonely existence. I walk the halls with my head down and a lump in my throat, feeling invisible. Occasionally, I'll text with Eve and Mallory, letting them know how busy I am with new friends and after-school activities. They seem to buy my lies. Dylan, meanwhile, is actually living the life I describe — joining a skateboarding club and always racing to answer his buzzing phone — which makes the whole thing more painful.

The Dark Ones weigh on my mind, too. There are no more screams or attacks, but everyone seems on edge after what happened to Mr. Bernal. On Wednesday, the principal makes an announcement that the janitor is "taking a leave of absence and will be out for the remainder of the school year."

Rumors zip around: Some students whisper that he was bitten by a rabid dog, and others argue that he did go crazy. In gym class, I overhear two jock guys debating the topic. One says, "Dude, what if Mr. B was attacked by a *vampire*?" I freeze, and the other guy replies, "Dude, that's ridiculous. You watch too much TV."

If only they knew.

When the final bell rings on Thursday, though, all thoughts of Mr. Bernal leave my head. I sprint out of science class, stop at my locker, and head to the bathroom where I bat-shifted on Monday. Luckily, I haven't shifted again since then. And this time, I'm here for a different kind of quick change.

That morning, my skin was still a little red and

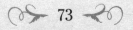

sore, so I wore my usual long-sleeved shirt and jeans. But now, a glance in the mirror confirms that my sunburn is much better. Even the bump on my forehead has gone down. So I step into the memorable stall and change into a fitted white tee, a pinstriped vest, a short denim skirt, and the same espadrilles that Paige owns. If I want to be the stylish wardrobe master, I need to look the part.

Then I stash my old clothes back in my locker and stride downstairs to the auditorium, feeling like a new woman.

The auditorium looks like how I'd imagine a movie set does, only without cameras. Mr. Harker is sitting in the front row with a notepad, his expression serious. A sixth-grade girl wearing a black T-shirt that reads PRODUCTION ASSISTANT is handing him a giant iced latte from The Coffee Bean. Students are clustered throughout the rows or onstage, reading thick bound scripts. Sasha, wearing a headset, is walking around and giving orders into the little microphone: "Marc, you have to adjust the spotlight in Act One. And tell the prop master we need one of the bat puppets replaced."

When Sasha spots me standing there, wide-eyed, she smirks and removes her headset. "Well," she says, a bit snarkily. "I'm surprised to see you here, considering you've been avoiding me all week."

I cross my arms over my chest, annoyed. "I was not avoiding you," I protest, even though I pretended I was hard of hearing whenever she said hello to me in homeroom. And looked the other way whenever her brother waved at me in the hall.

What I really want to say is, *I'm not here for you*, but it's clear that Sasha wields some power in this play, so I hold my tongue.

"Okay," she replies, shrugging. "Come on, I'll take you to Mr. Harker. When he's sitting like that with his notepad, he's in 'the zone,' so you need to approach him carefully." She shakes her head, her curls bouncing.

"It's all so . . . professional," I say in awe as we walk past Carmen, who is hunched over her script and furiously highlighting some lines.

"No kidding," Sasha says. "Mr. Harker was a child actor — he was in a bunch of movies and commercials and stuff — so he has a lot of experience. And S.M.A. in general takes theater very seriously. On opening night, there are always producers and directors and casting agents in the audience. It's a big deal."

I feel a shiver of anticipation. So this isn't just some ordinary middle school production. It's very *Hollywood*. That makes me even more determined to be a part of it.

"Excuse us, Mr. Harker," Sasha says softly, and the director looks up from his notepad, his glasses askew. I bite my lip, intimidated, but then he smiles.

"Ah, Ashlee!" he says. "Excellent. Let's go backstage so I can show you what we're working with for the costumes. Sasha," he adds, "will you please let the cast members know that we'll be starting rehearsal in about ten minutes?"

Sasha nods, putting her headset back on. I realize that, in spite of her baggy hot-pink tunic, zebra-print leggings, and giant gold hoop earrings, Mr. Harker sees Sasha as very competent and responsible. I'm sort of impressed.

I follow Mr. Harker behind the velvet curtain to the dark backstage area. It smells musty and ancient. A crooked hallway leads to what look like dressing rooms and supply closets. There's a ladder, a long rope, and a bag overflowing with painted masks. In the shadows, these items seem menacing, and I step carefully to keep from stumbling. The thought pops into my head that, as a bat, I'd be able to get around here fine.

I hear a rustle, sort of like wings, behind me. I shudder. What if there *is* a bat back here — *the* bat that attacked Mr. Bernal?

"Look out, Ashlee!" a voice calls out from above, and I skitter to a stop, my breath catching. I glance up and see a glass booth perched high above Mr. Harker and me. Marc is inside it, sitting in front of a panel of knobs and switches. Gordon is beside him, wearing a big pair of headphones and, as usual, typing on his laptop.

"You almost bumped into that mannequin," Marc tells me.

"*What* mannequin?" I ask. I face forward again — and stare right at a headless figure. I cover my mouth to keep from crying out.

"Yep, that's the one," Marc snorts, then bursts out laughing. What a jerk!

Mr. Harker frowns up at Marc, then turns to me. "This is a dressmaker's dummy you can use for sizing costumes," Mr. Harker explains.

"What's this about costumes?" Paige demands, stepping out of the shadows with Wendy at her side.

Paige, in a cute plaid romper, is holding a bound script, and Wendy, in a short black dress and UGGs, is carrying a bag full of creepily real-looking bat puppets.

Paige takes in my own outfit, clearly surprised by how fashionable I look. I feel a small swell of triumph. Then her eyes land on my feet and she smirks, nudging Wendy.

"Wow, real original choice in footwear, Rash," Paige sneers. "I guess imitation *is* the sincerest form of flattery, though."

A searing heat races through me, and I clench my fists. She's not going to make this easy, is she?

"Paige, Wendy, I was hoping to find you," Mr. Harker says. "Ashlee would like to be the new wardrobe master, and we should all hear what she has in mind." To me, he adds, "Paige is playing Vera, and Wendy is our prop master. They had the strongest opinions about Ellen, our former wardrobe master."

Wendy nods imperiously, and Paige continues to smirk at me, her eyes glinting.

Dread settles like a stone in my stomach. So this is some kind of . . . *audition*?

"Here's our costume supply room," Wendy says in a brisk voice, opening a door next to the mannequin. "What do you think?"

Inside are endless racks of clothing, along with shoes, scarves, feather boas, and hats. There are satin ball gowns, tuxedos, soldiers' uniforms, tutus, regular jeans and tees . . . the works. I gulp, overwhelmed. But I need to keep calm. Otherwise, I could bat-shift.

"This should be interesting," I hear Paige murmur, and that gives me all the resolve I need to step inside.

"O-okay," I stammer, reaching into my satchel and taking out my notebook. I flip through the pages, scanning the ideas I wrote down. "In the movie, Vera wears a lot of lace," I begin, "so that could be cool to incorporate into the play. Like . . . this." I pull a white high-collared lace dress off one of the rods. If I pretend I'm working at a fashion magazine, helping Arabella, this seems easier. Even fun.

"That's pretty," I hear Wendy whisper to Paige, who nudges her again.

"And Vera's very naive," I go on, feeling a bit more confident. "Mr. Harker said in English class on Monday that the color green sometimes represents innocence."

"So?" Paige yawns, and I'm sure she's thinking I'm a kiss-up.

"So . . ." I spot a gorgeous emerald green gown and take it down from the rod. "Vera could wear a lot

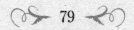

of green. She could even wear this the night she finds Vladimir, um, you know, sucking Mila's blood."

I blush, hating how close this play hits to home.

"Paigey, that would look amazing on you!" Wendy exclaims, quickly glancing at her friend for approval.

Paige's smirk has disappeared, and now she's eyeing me in a careful, cunning way. As if she no longer knows what to make of me.

"Hmm," she says at last. "Not a bad start, Rash-lee."

I let out a breath I didn't even know I'd been holding.

"Definitely better than Ellen, right?" Wendy says, and grudgingly, Paige nods.

I hug the dresses to me, full of cautious excitement. *It's happening!*

"I agree," Mr. Harker says. "Any thoughts on Vladimir's costumes, Ashlee?"

"Well, the cape he wears in the movie is sort of clichéd for a vampire," I explain, casting my eyes down as I speak the *V* word. "Maybe he could wear a dark suit instead?"

"Good idea," Mr. Harker says. "I think you're a natural, Ashlee. Welcome aboard!" Paige opens her mouth, possibly to protest, but Mr. Harker adds,

"Now, it's high time we started rehearsing. Ashlee, you should come watch."

I can't stop grinning as I replace the dresses and float out of the costume room. I don't even look up at Marc and Gordon in the sound booth. Then I join Mr. Harker and Sasha in the front row as the actors take their places onstage.

"Are you in?" Sasha asks me, and I nod, too happy to bother blowing her off.

"I bet a certain someone will be glad about that," Sasha replies, smiling to herself.

Who? I wonder, mystified. Paige? She didn't seem glad, though I'm sure she'll come around. Wendy? Before I can ask, the lights dim, and the rehearsal starts.

A spotlight shines down, and Paige steps into it. "The year was 1789," she begins in a weird accent. It sounds like a mix between Valley Girl and Eastern European ballerina. "I went to — I mean, I — um. Line, please?" she snaps, glancing at Sasha.

I look over at Sasha, too. She doesn't even need to consult the script in her lap. "I traveled to Transylvania to meet . . ." she prompts.

"To meet, um, a wealthy landowner named Vladimir," Paige finishes quickly.

I cringe. Paige is *terrible*. She may be poised and pretty, but she can't act for the life of her.

"Paige, can we start over?" Mr. Harker asks in a weary voice. "Maybe without the accent this time?"

Paige rolls her eyes but she tries again, sounding somewhat better. As the rehearsal goes on, I notice that she messes up her lines a lot, while the other actors have theirs memorized. The boy who plays Vladimir, James Okada (I recognize him as one of the cute boys from the popular lunch table), is actually really good. And Carmen, who plays Mila, is decent, too. Paige is the only weak spot.

I'd do a better job, I catch myself thinking, then dismiss the idea. I'm wardrobe master, not an actor, which is for the best. Parents and other audience members will surely film the play and take photos. And a big blank spot onstage would definitely raise some questions.

Plus, trying to steal the lead role from Paige would kind of ruin my plan to become her BFF.

"Awful, huh?" Sasha whispers to me at one point. Although Sasha's idea of whispering is practically like shouting. "I mean, I just want to speak her lines *for* her."

"Shh," I respond. Though I secretly agree with Sasha, I'm not going to admit it.

But then the fake bats — courtesy of Wendy — are released from backstage, and Paige is supposed to faint. She trips forward, lands on her knees, and plants her face on the stage, all in slow motion. I squirm, bothered by the bats — another reminder that this story mirrors my life — and Paige's sorry attempt at passing out. Having done it myself recently, I can say it's very different.

"That didn't look too realistic, Paige," Mr. Harker says.

She sits up, pouting. "What do you mean?" she asks darkly.

"I thought it was great, Paigey!" Carmen pipes up, stepping onto the stage.

I can't stop myself from speaking. "Maybe you should fall backward instead?" I suggest. I'm trying to be helpful, but Paige shoots daggers at me.

"It was the music," she says angrily, pointing up at the control booth. "The cues are *all* off."

Mr. Harker sighs and asks Paige to try again. I seal my lips shut, vowing to keep my critiques to myself from now on.

Finally, Carmen pretends to die, James pretends to bite Paige's neck, and then a big crescent moon dangles down, along with two bat puppets. *Ta-da!* Sasha and I clap, but Mr. Harker shakes his head, murmuring something about "lots more work to be done." He asks the cast and crew to gather around.

"Next week is a short one because of Martin Luther King Day on Monday," he explains. "So I'm moving up our next rehearsal to lunchtime on Tuesday. It's crucial that we improve in time for opening night on Friday."

"Yeah," Paige speaks up, flipping her hair over one shoulder. "Some people in the *crew* need to get their music cues right." She glares at Gordon, who shrugs helplessly. Marc, for once, isn't by his side.

"We should also do the fittings on Tuesday," Mr. Harker says to me. "That way, we can send the costumes to the dry cleaners in case they need to be resized. Ashlee, are you able to go to the costume room now and make your selections?"

I nod, feeling very official. Even if Paige's performance is bad, I can make sure she *looks* perfect.

Sasha hands me an extra script to use for reference, and as people gather up their bags, I head backstage. I'll have to be quick; I need to be home in time for dinner, since Mom isn't filming for once. I'm also starting to crave a Sanga!

It's even quieter and darker here now, and I make a point of walking right around the headless manne-quin. I glance up at the control booth to make sure Marc isn't laughing at me, but there's no one in there. Weird. I wonder where he went.

I'm opening the door to the costume room when I hear a strange sound. Not rustling this time, but more like . . . something being dragged.

My heart thumps as I turn and peer down the crooked hallway. There, in a slim shaft of light com-ing from the stage, I see Marc. He's pulling a large white-and-red cooler out of a supply closet.

A very familiar-looking cooler.

Where did you get that? I want to scream. *Whose is it?*

But I can't speak, or even move. I can only stare, my throat dry, as Marc kneels down and opens the cooler. He glances around furtively — it's obvious he has no idea I'm right there — and takes out a very familiar-looking cup filled with red liquid.

Then, with the ease of someone who has done it many times before, he inserts a straw and takes a long drink.

I gasp. Then, for the second time that afternoon, I clamp my hand over my mouth to keep silent. Soundlessly, I slip inside the costume room. I stand amid the colorful clothes, dizzy, until I hear Marc stash the cooler away. I listen as he walks out onto the stage, saying hi to Gordon.

As if everything is normal. As if *he's* normal.

But he's not.

Marc Hirsh was drinking Sanga!, which can only mean one thing:

Marc Hirsh is a vampire.

Chapter Seven

I'm in a state of shock. Somehow, with trembling hands and a racing pulse, I manage to select the costumes for each scene and set them aside for Tuesday. Then I walk out of the empty auditorium and leave the school.

As twilight falls, I cut home through the bustling Third Street Promenade, passing the Apple Store and American Apparel. But not even the new skirts on display at J. Crew appeal to me. My thoughts are tumbling and twisting, toppling over each other.

Marc. How can it be? I don't remember him from the initiation ceremony in New York. True, there were so many kids there, all clustered in a pitch-dark room, and I'd been too scared to study their faces.

What about Sasha? Is *she* a vampire, too? Maybe there's a rule about twins. I really need to read the Handbook.

And do Sasha and Marc suspect the truth about me? There's no way they could, right? I'm not as careless as Marc, bringing a whole Sanga! cooler to school.

Or maybe, I think as I walk past palm trees tilting in the breeze, *I saw wrong*. Maybe it wasn't Sanga! he was drinking but some juice. *I'd* been wanting a Sanga!, so it was on my mind. After all, there have been no other signs giving Marc away. I can't even picture him shifting into a bat.

I unlock the door to our house — Vladimir's castle — and kick off my espadrilles. As I climb the stairs to my room, one last thought, slippery and darker than the others, weasels its way into my head. If Marc *is* a vampire, maybe *he's* the Dark One who attacked Mr. Bernal!

I remember how, at lunch on Monday, Marc showed up in the cafeteria late. He'd told Sasha he'd had something to do. Was that too much of a coincidence?

I have to tell Arabella that there's a suspect. In my room, I call her, but I get her voice mail. I text her — Dark Ones update!! — but she doesn't text back. I e-mail her and get a bounce-back message that says she's away from her desk, dealing with a Fashion Week crisis. Frustrated, I bang my hand on my own desk. *I'm* having a crisis! What if I was in serious danger from a Dark One?

I guess my mentor would be too busy partying with Calvin Klein to care.

"So what's new with you?" Dylan asks me smugly over our dinner of chicken tacos from Baja Fresh. He's finished telling Mom and me about a party he's invited to in Malibu this weekend. I can tell he's loving our recent role reversal.

I lift my chin and tell him and Mom the truth, that I'm now wardrobe master of the seventh-grade play. Dylan seems impressed, especially when I explain that it's an adaptation of *At First Bite*. But Mom gives a small frown.

"I would hope you'd at least get to be onstage," she says as she reaches for the guacamole. "Maybe even as an understudy? I'm sure you'd be *perfect*."

I sigh, wishing I could tell my mother the truth about me and at the same time wishing she would leave me alone. "It's a great position," I finally respond. "I hope you'll come to the opening night next Friday."

"It depends," Mom says. "We're supposed to be filming late that day. I'll see what I can do."

Before bed, as I'm preparing a Paige-worthy outfit for tomorrow, I get a text back from Arabella. At last!

What's up, Ash? it reads, and I can almost hear her impatience through the words. Was there another attack??

Feeling a little sheepish, I write:

No. But I think there's a vampire in my grade. Could possibly b a Dark 1.

Arabella responds quickly:

OK. Don't jump 2 any conclusions, tho. Am going off the grid 4 a few days. Too much work & boyfriend's bday. XOXO.

I sigh and crawl onto my air mattress. So my mentor's not going to be much help. But I do have somewhere else I can go for answers. Flicking on my bedside lamp, I crack open the Vampire's Handbook. A plume of dust rises up from the first page, reminding me that I've barely glanced at the book since November.

I skim the Table of Contents. *Chapter One: Adjusting to Your New Life. Chapter Two: The Art of Bat-Shifting. Chapter Three: Identifying a Fellow Vampire.*

Aha! I flip to Chapter Three, knowing that I really need to study Chapter Two at some point. Chapter Three has a long list of factors that I'm already all too familiar with — *skin cold to the touch*; *invisibility in photographs*; *sensitivity to the sun.* There's one part that notes that siblings and fraternal twins are rarely both vampires, so that probably rules out Sasha.

It also says that though vampires are secretive, they will admit their condition to another vampire if asked.

Okay. I decide that tomorrow, I'll gather my courage, corner Marc in the hallway, and demand: *Are you, or are you not, a vampire?* If it turns out I'm wrong, I'll just laugh and say working on the play is giving me ideas. And if I'm right . . . well, I don't know. I'll have to wing it. Like a bat. I smirk then shut off the light.

But on Friday, I can't put my plan into action. In homeroom, I hear Sasha telling Gordon that Marc is sick and stayed at home.

"He came down with a cold after rehearsal," she's saying as I take my seat. "I hope I don't catch it."

I'm so intent on eavesdropping that I almost miss Paige, Carmen, and Wendy walking right by my desk.

"Hey," Paige says pointedly, nodding at me. Carmen and Wendy nod as well.

I'm stunned. *Paige acknowledged me!* And she didn't call me Rash-lee. I can't help the smile that spreads over my face. I knew becoming wardrobe master was the right move. I even notice Carmen cast an admiring glance at my Tory Burch flats as she takes her seat. It's all I can do not to clap and cheer. I'm so close to being where I want to be.

"That's too bad," Gordon is saying to Sasha. "He's supposed to meet me at noon tomorrow at the Apple Store."

"Maybe he'll be better by then," Sasha replies.

I remember something Arabella said to me on Monday night: that Dark Ones who go too long without human blood can get sick. It's been several days since the attack on Mr. Bernal, so if Marc is really a Dark One, there will be another attack . . . soon.

On Saturday, I sleep in. Our furniture finally arrived last night, so I luxuriate in my big, comfy bed. The long weekend stretches out ahead of me. Back in New York, I know, Eve and Mallory will be shopping at Bloomingdale's, but for once, I don't feel like I'm missing out. There are plenty of things to do here in LA, like seeing the Hollywood Walk of Fame, or, as Mom suggested last night, hitting up Rodeo Drive.

I'm about to go downstairs and remind Mom of these plans when the wail of sirens outside makes me jump. I realize then that I'd been hearing the sirens, distantly, all morning. But in my fog of drows-iness, I didn't pay attention.

I slip on my terry-cloth sweatpants, pink hoodie, and flip-flops before stepping out onto my balcony. It's an overcast, slightly chilly day. But the air still smells sweet, like flowers and oranges. Across the street, by the entrance to the beach, I see police cars, news vans, and a crowd of concerned-looking people.

A finger of worry pokes me. It could be a shark sighting, or maybe a skateboarder fell and skinned his knee (is it so wrong of me to picture Dylan?). But a niggling feeling in my gut tells me it's something more sinister. Something that I'll find important.

I go over to my computer and pull up Google. I type in *Santa Monica* and the word *attack*. A second later, a news item pops up. The headline makes my jaw drop:

SURFER FOUND ON SANTA MONICA BEACH WITH SEVERE NECK WOUND; IN STABLE CONDITION AT HOSPITAL.

"Oh no," I whisper. My eyes dart over the article, taking in random phrases.

In what was believed to be a wild animal attack, a twenty-one-year-old surfer was bitten this morning. . . . The young man recalls "a dark, winged thing, like a bird, maybe" flying at him before he blacked out. . . .

He was found in an odd "frozen" state and suffered
significant blood loss but was able to communicate. . . .
Police have no leads.

I shrink backward in my chair, terror gripping my throat. There's no way this is a coincidence. Every detail is too similar to Mr. Bernal's attack. *I was right*, I think as I stand up in a panic. *Marc was sick, and he attacked again.* It makes sense that he'd hunt someone on the beach, since that's clearly a place he hangs out.

Somehow I feel responsible, as if I should have done something to prevent this. As if I need to do something now.

I glance wildly around my room. I could text Arabella, but it's unlikely she'd get back to me. I could call the police, but then I'd run the risk of everyone discovering *I'm* a vampire. I could look in the Handbook, but I don't even know where I put it — a lot of stuff got misplaced last night in the shuffle of moving in my furniture. I could — I could — I close my eyes, overwhelmed. Then, in the next instant, there's nothing I *can* do.

Because I'm transforming into a bat.

I know I shouldn't have panicked. But it's too late. My teeth have already lengthened into sharp fangs, and my body is shrinking upward as my arms become wings. I feel my eyes burn red and my claws take shape. I'm morphing much faster than I ever have before. Within seconds, the mirror on my wall shows a bat in my bedroom.

At least, I console myself, I'm alone. I'm not in school, or with friends, and there's no one I have to hide from. . . .

"Ashlee?"

Except for my mother.

I hear her coming down the hall and can smell her expensive moisturizing cream.

"Ashlee, I hope you're not still sleeping," she says in a singsong. "It's almost noon, and I was thinking we could go shopping on Rodeo Drive!"

I flash to an image of my mom, impeccably dressed and groomed, walking into Chanel with a bat perched on her shoulder. I almost want to laugh.

I hear Mom's hand on the doorknob. I'm reminded of my last night in New York, when Arabella narrowly escaped by flying out my window. . . .

I glance at the still-open doors to my terrace. I take a breath, flap my wings, and propel myself outside, into the cool air. I hear Mom entering my now-empty room. "She must have gone to the beach," she murmurs to herself. "I hope she wore sunscreen."

I do fly toward the beach, since it's straight ahead. Although it's not sunny, there are a few people dotting the sand. It's bizarre — and a teeny bit cool — to see them beneath me: little colorful figures lying out on towels. Then I see a group of police officers and realize I'm in danger. The surfer said he was attacked by a "dark, winged thing." If someone happens to glance up at the sky, they'll see just that. They'll see me.

I can't linger here. And I can't go home either, since Mom could still be in my room. I hover for a moment, thinking, and then it hits me: In homeroom yesterday, Gordon said he and Marc were meeting at the Apple Store at noon. I'm not far from the Third Street Promenade. If I head over there, I can check to see if Marc is healthy-looking again — and maybe I can pick up some other clues, too.

Suddenly, for the first time ever, I'm glad that I'm in bat form. It will give me the chance to move quickly and spy on Marc, as long as he doesn't look up.

I make an abrupt turn, and my stomach does a weird swooping thing, kind of like the time I rode the roller coaster at Coney Island with Eve. But I keep flying ahead. I've never been in bat form outside during the daytime, and it feels sort of nice to have the wind in my face. Yes, I'm worried that any minute I'll shift back and fall out of the sky. But behind my fear is a sense of freedom and wonder. I'm as tall as the palm trees!

The Third Street Promenade is crowded with shoppers. My gaze scans over parents, toddlers, elderly couples . . . and then lands on a boy about my age, with curly dark hair. He's really here, wearing his S.M.A. BEARS shirt and making his way toward the Apple Store.

Marc, the Dark One.

He does look healthy, strolling along as if he didn't commit a horrific act this morning. The human blood must have cured him. I gnash my teeth in anger, convinced of his guilt.

Without thinking, I swoosh down low, and as Marc opens the door, I follow him inside. I'm totally concentrated on my target, watching as he walks —

"Bat!" someone screams at top volume.

"Oh my God, how did it get in?"

"Catch it!"

It takes me a split second to understand that the object of everyone's freak-out is me. How could I have been so stupid? My heart pounds as I zoom around, desperate to escape. Some shrieking person is holding the door open, and I shoot through it and back onto the street. I notice a shaggy palm tree nearby and I dart behind it, shaking.

You need to shift back, I tell myself. The angry Apple hordes could be on their way to find me. *Close your eyes, breathe, and imagine yourself shifting back. Just do it.*

And somehow, I do. My legs begin to lengthen out, and my claws uncurl and become feet again. My hair spills over my shoulders as my face returns to normal size.

I draw in a steadying breath and look down at myself, taking stock. I appear to be a twelve-year-old girl again, back in my sweatpants, hoodie, and flip-flops. I did it! I actually controlled my shifting back. I smile in disbelief, and relief. Does this mean that one day I'll be able to control my bat-shifting? I can only hope so. Either way, I have to tell Arabella!

Still cautious, I step out from behind the palm tree. It doesn't seem like anyone from the Apple Store has chased me; they probably were just glad to see the bat leave. I feel a swell of pride, and I stride back to the store. I might not be in disguise anymore, but I can still spy on Marc from a distance.

I'm reaching for the door when someone taps me on the shoulder.

"How's your forehead, dear?"

I give a start, then turn to see a pudgy woman smiling at me. She's wearing slacks and a T-shirt, not light blue scrubs, so it takes me a second to realize it's Nurse Murray.

"Oh — better," I reply, caught off guard. It's always weird to see your teachers out of school. And I don't feel like making awkward conversation right now. I'm still calming down from my bat-shift.

"Glad to hear it," Nurse Murray replies sunnily. "It seems the whole world is getting into accidents," she adds, her expression growing serious. "Did you hear about that poor surfer this morning? Sounded an awful lot like what happened to our Mr. Bernal, didn't it?"

I feel a funny tingle. I think back to Mr. Bernal's attack and that red spot near Nurse Murray's mouth. I study her closely now. Why would she specifically bring up this morning's incident? And why is she hanging out near the beach today, anyway?

I narrow my eyes. Maybe Marc isn't the one I should be following after all. . . .

"Well, I'll let you enjoy your day, dear," Nurse Murray says, perhaps flustered by my penetrating stare. She waggles her fingers at me.

Feeling confused, I watch her walk off. Should I trail her to find out where she's going? Stay here? I glance behind me into the Apple Store. I could swear I see Marc by the door. Can he see me, too? My heart leaps, and I hurry a few paces away, blending into the crowd.

I feel drained. I'm hungry, and Mom must be wondering why I've been gone so long. Maybe it's time to give my spy mission a rest. So, zipping up my hoodie, I head for home. I've already had more than enough excitement to last me the whole long weekend.

Chapter Eight

"How was your weekend?"

In homeroom on Tuesday, I look up to see Paige standing by my desk. Carmen and Wendy are on either side of her, like pretty bodyguards. But today, the girls don't seem menacing or cruel. Instead, they seem like they're simply saying hello . . .

To me!

I try not to grin too wide.

"It was fine," I say breezily. I decide it best not to bring up my little flight to the Third Street Promenade. "My mom and I went to Rodeo Drive." I tap my new blue-and-red charm bracelet. After the insanity on Saturday, I needed some retail therapy.

"Oh." Paige purses her lips, and dimples appear in her cheeks. "See, *we* always shop at the Beverly

Center or Fred Segal. Rodeo Drive is too touristy." I nod, crestfallen, but Paige adds, "No worries. You'll get the hang of it soon."

My heart surges with hope.

"That's supercute, BTW," Carmen says, pointing at my bracelet. I beam.

"See you at lunchtime rehearsal," Paige says to me as she, Carmen, and Wendy head for their desks. "I'll be there early for the costume fittings!"

"Can't wait!" I reply, then bite my lip. Did that sound too eager?

"I can," Sasha mutters. I blink at her; I didn't even notice her sit down as I was chatting with the girls. "I guarantee Paige will have a zillion complaints about the costumes and be as annoying as ever."

"No, she won't," I snap. Paige is already pleased with my costume picks. Why would she change her mind?

I glare at Sasha. I wonder what she knows about her brother and his whereabouts early Saturday morning. I'm still no closer to figuring out the identity of the Dark One. Over the weekend, there were no other attacks reported on the news, and the wounded surfer was said to be recovering at the hospital.

Though I texted Arabella about the beach attack — and my successful shifting — I heard nothing from her. I'm starting to think that I'm on my own in this investigation. I'll have to keep a careful eye out for both Marc and Nurse Murray today.

Mr. Harker comes in then, full of energy. After taking attendance, he shows the class the amazing posters he had printed up for the play. They're red and black, with a big crescent moon in the background. He says the sixth-grade production assistants will be hanging them up around the school and in town.

I feel a burst of excitement and momentarily forget about Dark Ones. Last night, I went on a bunch of fashion and costume design blogs for inspiration. One explained that measuring tape and scissors are always necessary at costume fittings. I packed my bag accordingly, and feel like a true wardrobe master now.

My good mood lasts through the morning. I don't even mind when I pass Dylan in the hallway, his arm around a beautiful high school girl. I almost wave to him but catch myself, remembering our rule. Soon enough, though, I'll be as socially secure as my doofus brother. If I play my cards right, by opening night I'll be in the popular crowd.

When the lunch bell rings, I'm craving a Sanga! like crazy. So I duck into an empty study room in the library and gulp my drink as quickly as I can. Then I sprint down to the auditorium, praying I won't be late.

Of course, I'm the first to arrive. Catching my breath, I take off my cardigan and twist my hair up into a bun. Then I plunk my bag down in an empty row, remove my tape measure, scissors, and notebook, and head backstage.

It's deserted here, too, except for the headless mannequin. I peer up at the control booth and down the narrow hall, but there's no sign of Marc. Good. I can't deal with seeing him yet. I march purposefully toward the costume room; I need to be in there, ready to take measurements, once the cast arrives.

I push open the door, and the world falls away.

Paige is lying frozen on the floor, right beneath Vera's green gown. Her golden curls fan out behind her, and her big blue eyes stare up at the ceiling. Spots of red bloom on her neck: two small, awful punctures. Fang marks.

I open my mouth to scream but no sound comes out.

Paige was attacked by the Dark One!

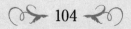

104

I stumble toward Paige's motionless body and kneel beside her. The items I was carrying clatter onto the floor. I touch Paige's wrist and her pulse ticks faintly. My own pulse is tap-dancing wildly. I need to go get help, but now it's like I'm frozen, too.

I can't believe that this morning Paige was talking snippily about Rodeo Drive. Now she's as limp as a rag doll. Her iPhone lies in one hand, and her mouth sags open. Was she going to phone someone for help when she saw the bat?

And *who* was the bat? Did Nurse Murray find her way back here, looking for fresh blood? We're not too far from her office. Or was Marc conveniently hanging out backstage when he came upon his next victim?

I make myself speak. "Paige?" I say, lightly shaking her shoulder. "What happened?"

Paige blinks and slowly lifts her head. I feel a wave of relief. She looks at me, confused, and whispers, "Ashlee?"

"Yes, it's me," I say. "Do you remember who attacked you?"

But Paige can only stare at me with hollow eyes. Then, weakly, she puts her head down on the dusty floor again.

I hear the voices of the cast members right outside the door. I swallow hard. Do I tell them what happened to Paige? Or do I keep quiet about my knowledge of fang marks and dark, winged things?

Before I can decide, the cast streams inside, led by Carmen.

"Okay, Ashlee," she is saying, "I hope you picked some good dresses for Mila. . . ."

The words die on her lips as her eyes bug out of her head. Behind her, the whole cast falls silent.

Then Carmen lets out an earsplitting wail.

"Paigey! No!" she cries, bolting forward and flinging herself down next to her friend. "Oh my God! Are you alive? Paigey, what's wrong with you? Please!"

Gasps and shrieks erupt from the rest of the cast. As if irritated by the hysterics, Paige sighs and closes her eyes.

"It's just like Mr. Bernal!" James Okada shouts.

"I heard about a surfer who got stabbed in the neck on Saturday," the girl who plays Vera's mother murmurs.

Not stabbed, I think, but don't say.

"We need help!" hollers the boy who plays Vera's father.

In an instant, most of the crew, including Sasha, Marc, and Gordon, barrel in. Sasha looks worried, Gordon looks distracted as ever, and Marc looks — stricken. His eyebrows are furrowed and he's frowning. Is it because he's feeling guilty?

"What's going on?" Mr. Harker demands, striding in with Wendy at his heels. When he sees Paige on the ground, he hurries over to her. "Nobody panic," he instructs, although everyone is doing just that.

Carmen is now sobbing and clinging to her friend. My fingers are still glued to Paige's wrist. Mr. Harker steps around Carmen and gently moves me aside so he can kneel by Paige. His hands are cold, so I can tell he's as scared as the rest of us. As a teacher, though, he has to hide it.

He feels Paige's pulse. "Please go get Nurse Murray," he tells a sixth-grade production assistant. She nods and takes off at a run.

Paige's long lashes flutter open, and she coughs. She looks from Carmen to Mr. Harker to me. "Ashlee?" she croaks. It's all she seems capable of saying.

Carmen glares at me. "Why did she say *your* name?" she demands.

"Because I — I found her," I stammer. "Like this."

"Did you?" Wendy asks, her voice cold and sharp. I was expecting her to have a meltdown like Carmen, but her eyes look steely. "Isn't that interesting, Ashlee?"

I'm surprised by her tone. I'd always suspected that Wendy was the sweetest of the bunch and maybe even secretly liked me.

"What are you *talking* about?" I ask her. I feel my whole body tremble. *Do not bat-shift*, I tell myself firmly.

"Paige had just texted me," Wendy says, holding up her cell phone. "She came to check out the costumes before everyone else and decided she didn't like *any* of your choices after all, Ashlee."

"She did?" I glance at the iPhone in Paige's hand, feeling betrayed. So Sasha had been right. I look for her in the crowd, and she's watching me, her hazel eyes wide.

"Oh, yes," Wendy says crisply. "And *I* believe that when you came in, she told you her opinion. You got furious and attacked her," she finishes, sounding like a TV detective. "Look!" she adds, and points to the scissors on the floor beside me. "You used those as the weapon. You even have blood on your hands."

"No — I —" I look down and see that some Sanga! splashed onto my fingers. My stomach goes rock-cold.

The cast and crew murmur all around me. Do they believe what Wendy is saying? Do they think I'm capable of such a crime?

"No!" I exclaim. I get to my feet as Mr. Harker continues to take Paige's pulse and Carmen continues to weep into her friend's shoulder. "You don't understand. This isn't blood — it's — it's something else, and Paige was already frozen when I walked in."

Wendy shrugs. "I'm just saying you're the only one with a motive, that's all."

"You're wrong, Wendy!" Carmen cuts in, lifting her tearstained face. I'm about to thank her, until she continues. "Ashlee didn't do it because of the costumes," she says heatedly. "She did it because she wanted Paige out of the play. So *she* could get the lead role instead." Carmen whips her head around toward me. "You said on your first day here that you live in the house where *At First Bite* was filmed. And you critiqued Paige's performance during rehearsal. You even kind of look like Paige . . . and like Vera . . . so you want to be the star!"

There's a horrible, gaping silence followed by

more whispers. Wendy nods at Carmen, as if this new theory is a better one. Not even Mr. Harker leaps to my defense.

I'm speechless. Yes, the thought of playing Vera had crossed my mind — and it would certainly make my mother happy. But I did not do this to Paige. I would not do this to anyone. And I wasn't passed out somewhere this time. There's no gap in my memory. *I am not a Dark One.*

I want to defend myself, but a lump is forming in my throat and my vision is starting to blur with tears.

So much for making it into the popular crowd.

Then a voice, loud and clear, carries across the room.

"You guys are being ridiculous," Sasha snaps. "Ashlee didn't do anything. You're just pinning this on her because she's the new girl. Plus, Paige would be in much worse shape if she'd been attacked with *scissors.* Think about it." She rolls her eyes.

Gratitude washes over me. I almost want to run over to Sasha and throw my arms around her. Almost.

"Good point," James says. "Paige looks like Mr. Bernal did last week when they found him. And didn't he say something about a bat? Hey," he adds, glancing at Wendy. "We have fake bats in the play. Maybe it's a publicity stunt or something?"

"Of course it's not," Wendy replies sharply. "We would know about that."

If only the attacks were nothing but stunts. Unfortunately, they're all too real.

But thanks to Sasha and James, I find the courage I was missing a few moments ago. I blink back my tears and clear my throat.

"I think you're on the right track, though," I tell James. "Paige's wound was obviously made by a pair of fan —"

"Oh, you're back!" Mr. Harker says. He's talking to the production assistant, who's just returned, out of breath.

"Nurse Murray's not in," she explains, fanning herself. "She took a personal day to go to a casting call for a reality show."

"Seriously?" Mr. Harker asks, shaking his head. "That seems unprofessional."

Nurse Murray being unprofessional is the last thing I care about. What matters is that she's been away from school all day. I stare at Marc, who is looking at the floor, as if deep in thought.

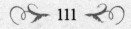

Nurse Murray was nowhere near the auditorium, I think, my heart thudding. *But Marc could have been....*

"There's a substitute nurse," the production assistant explains. "He asked if we could bring Paige to the office, since there's no gurney or anything."

"Of course. I'll need help, people," Mr. Harker says, bending down to sit Paige up. James, Gordon, and a few other guys rush forward to lend Mr. Harker a hand. I notice that Marc hangs back. Of course.

"Obviously, rehearsal's canceled," Mr. Harker says as he and the guys lift Paige to her feet. "We'll reconvene tomorrow at the usual time after school."

Paige's eyes are still open but her head droops. As the guys and Mr. Harker half-walk, half-carry her out of the costume room, I hear her mumbling, "Where am I? Where's the blackbird?"

I guess she doesn't remember any more than the other victims.

Carmen scrambles to her feet and rushes over to Wendy. The girls embrace, comforting each other loudly. I can't help but feel annoyed. I'd love to see how they'd react if they had to bat-shift. For them, vampires are all about drama and make-believe.

They will never understand my life.

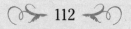

The girls must feel the intensity of my gaze, because they turn toward me and scowl. I scowl back. Then they link arms and scurry out of the room. I know they still think I'm behind Paige's injury, and there's a good chance that others are on their side.

Which makes me all the more determined to confront the real culprit.

By now, most everyone has left, following Paige en masse to the nurse's office. As Sasha and Marc turn to go, Sasha looks back at me.

"You okay?" she asks, and I nod, keeping my eyes on Marc.

When they're gone, I stash my innocent scissors, as well as my tape measure and notebook, on a spare shelf. As I leave the room, I see Sasha in the wings with the frazzled production assistant while Marc heads down the narrow hallway toward the supply closet. *Why?* I wonder, balling my hands into fists. Didn't he drink his fill?

I try to walk behind him as noiselessly as possible. My heart is pounding even harder now. But when I feel ready, I speak.

"I know what you are."

He turns around, one eyebrow raised. "Excuse me?" he asks.

"I know what you are," I repeat, my palms growing clammy. "I saw you drinking Sanga! backstage
last week. And," I go on, dropping my voice to a whisper, "I know what you did. To Paige. To the surfer. To
Mr. Bernal. Did you really think you could get away
with it?"

Boom.

Bomb dropped.

I stare right into his brown eyes, silently daring
him to lie or run away.

Marc doesn't flinch. Instead, he shrugs. And says:

"I know what you are, too. But I also know you're
not a Dark One. Neither am I. So why don't we put
our heads together and figure out who is?"

Chapter Nine

The hallway seems to tilt and wobble. Sweat breaks
out on my forehead and I take a few steps back from
Marc, almost crashing into the headless mannequin.

"How — how long have you known?" I ask, cross-
ing my arms over my chest.

The corner of his mouth lifts in a smile. "As soon
as I saw you that day on the beach. Only a vampire
would burn that badly, and that quickly. The same
thing happened to me the day after I became full-
fledged. SPF 75 is my friend."

I can't speak. My deepest, darkest secret is no
longer a secret. I came here to catch Marc off guard,
but he's somehow turned the tables on me.

"I knew for sure, though," Marc goes on, his eyes
sparkling, "when I saw the Sanga! cooler in your bag

at lunch. Remember? The time you almost tore off my arm trying to get the bag away from me?" He flashes me a grin, but I don't smile back. "I need to get one of those smaller coolers. I store mine in the prop closet. No one's ever seen me with it . . . except for you, of course."

I study Marc's face. I knew he was a vampire. But to hear him speak all these words — Sanga!, sunscreen, full-fledged — is startling and strange. I think back to all our previous interactions, my brain spinning. The beach, the cafeteria . . .

"Does Sasha know?" I whisper.

"No. I never told her my suspicions about you," Marc replies swiftly, and I exhale with relief. "But she knows about me, of course."

I feel my eyes widen. "She does? I thought we're not supposed to tell — you know, regular people. About us."

Marc shrugs again. "Sasha's my twin sister. She's an excellent secret-keeper. I'd trust her with my life."

I shake my head, thinking of Dylan. I can't imagine sharing this secret — or any secret — with him. Or my mom. Not to mention Eve or Mallory.

No wonder I've been feeling so lonely lately.

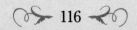

"What about Gordon?" I demand, and Marc shakes his head.

"It's tough, not being able to tell him," he says, a little sadly. "But he's so into his computer programming stuff. I don't think he even notices that I never want to iChat anymore. Or that I can smell what's for lunch before we even walk into school."

Like me! I think. I suddenly get the strangest sensation that someone, at last, understands me.

Hold on. What am I *thinking*? I narrow my eyes at Marc. I can't let my guard down.

"Okay. You trust Sasha. But why should I trust *you*?" I challenge. "Why should I believe you when you say you're not a Dark One?"

Marc holds my gaze, his expression serious. "There's no way I could be a Dark One, Ashlee," he says quietly. "My mother is on the Council, here in Los Angeles."

"She *is*?" I ask, blindsided. "You mean . . . your mom is a vampire, too?"

Marc nods. "She was really surprised when I got invited to the initiation ceremony in New York. Even though my skin had been getting cold and my teeth had been hurting since I turned twelve."

"Doesn't vampirism usually skip a generation or more?" I ask, thinking of my great-great-grandmother from Transylvania.

"Yeah, but not in our case," Marc replies. "And having a vampire mom sure makes the whole transition process easier, I'll tell you," he adds, his expression brightening. "I don't even need a mentor, since she fills that role. I think Sasha and my dad are a little jealous, to be honest."

I can't conceive of it. A family where vampirism is out in the open, where bat-shifting can be discussed at the dinner table. I have a million and one questions for Marc: What he thought of the initiation ceremony. Whether he has problems bat-shifting. What a typical day at the Hirsh home is like.

But I need to stay on topic.

"So, if your mom is on the Council," I say, trying to piece everything together. "She's, like, hunting Dark Ones? Or she'd know if you were one?"

"Have you read the Handbook?" Marc asks.

"Some of it," I reply defensively, tossing my hair. "I didn't really have the time before, and then I misplaced it in my room —"

"Anyway," Marc interrupts, fighting back a grin,

"if you had read it, then you'd know that Council members are routinely investigated by the Vampire Disciplinary Committee. It's to make sure no one in their families — or they themselves — are Dark Ones. So, you see, even if I *tried* to be a Dark One, my mom would get thrown off the Council . . . and I'd be grounded for eternity."

Oh.

Slowly, I drop my arms, but I remain a safe distance from Marc.

"If that's the case," I say, still suspicious, "why did you come to the cafeteria late the day Mr. Bernal was attacked? And then, you were sick on Friday, but you got better on Saturday, *right* after that surfer was attacked on the beach! It all made sense —"

Marc holds up his hands to stop me. "I was drinking Sanga! here, backstage, the day Mr. Bernal was attacked," he explains. "That's why I was late getting to the cafeteria. As for being sick, I happen to get over my colds quickly. Good immune system, I guess." He laughs, and I can't help but think he looks sort of cute when he does that. Ugh.

"Hey," he says, another grin tugging at his lips. "Did you know I was better on Saturday because you saw me at the Apple Store?"

"I — um —" I fidget, biting my lip and blushing. "Possibly."

Marc's face lights up, and he laughs again. "No way! You were that bat, weren't you? I guessed it when I saw you standing outside the store afterward!"

I glare at him, hating how my cheeks are burning. "Okay. Fine. I was that bat. You must be very *proud* of yourself for figuring everything out."

Marc shakes his head. "I wish I were better at figuring stuff out," he says grimly. "Then I'd know who was behind all these attacks."

There's a beat of silence, and finally, I take a tiny step closer to him.

"All right . . . so you're not a Dark One," I grudgingly admit. "But you must know a lot about them from your mom, right?"

"Dark Ones are tricky," Marc replies, furrowing his eyebrows and looking as thoughtful as he did back in the costume room. "They move around a lot, from country to country, or city to city, so it's hard for Council members to keep track of them. Also, they recruit new Dark Ones often, so a vampire who may have been totally ordinary before will suddenly, and without warning, start a series of attacks."

"Which sounds like what's happening now," I supply. Marc nods.

It's totally weird to be standing backstage with him, talking about all the things that have been haunting me lately. At the same time, though, it feels . . . good. Like I can finally confide in someone. Who knew it would be Marc?

"At the beginning of January," Marc explains, "rumors started going around that there were Dark Ones in Los Angeles. But now the Council knows it's true. There have been other attacks, too. My mom told me about one in Pasadena and another in Burbank. The local news will report it, but not much else gets done. We need to put a stop to this, before more people get hurt."

Marc sets his jaw, looking determined. I can't help thinking that he *is* cute, maybe even cuter than James Okada. But then I push the thought aside. *Focus, Ashlee.*

"Well, what's the next step?" I whisper. "I can try to call my mentor and get some answers, but —"

Before I can finish, the bell rings.

Right. We're in school. It's the end of lunchtime, and we have to get to class.

Marc seems to be processing the same thing. He blinks and glances back at the prop closet. "I should grab some Sanga! real quick," he says. "But listen — Ashlee — let's talk about this more." His cheeks turn red, and he ducks his head. "Would you, um, want to come to my house after school?" he asks.

I hesitate, fiddling with my new bracelet. On the one hand, I've found a vampire my own age who could help me solve the Dark Ones mystery. On the other hand, going to Marc and Sasha's house would mean that I was, like . . . a friend of theirs. In their group. All my hard work to fight my way into the popular crowd would be a waste. And while I'm on shaky ground with Carmen and Wendy right now, I can't throw in the towel yet. Not when I've made so much progress.

"I'm . . . I'm not sure," I finally respond, torn. "I'll think about it."

Disappointment flashes across Marc's face, and he shrugs. "Okay. But I don't think it's safe to talk about it in school anymore," he adds. "So text me or e-mail me if you have any updates. All my info's on the school directory."

"Same here," I say. Conflicting emotions battle inside me, but the late bell is about to ring. So I turn toward the wings.

"Ashlee?" Marc calls, and I look back at him. "Don't worry," he says, and gives me a charming half smile. "I won't tell Sasha or anyone else — about you. I promise."

And then we're off in opposite directions, two vampires with a lot on our minds.

I can't get to sleep that night. I call Arabella (no answer), and even call Eve and Mallory. I'm not sure what, if anything, I'm going to tell them, but they don't pick up, or call back. Typical. Then, while pacing my room, I spot my Handbook, wedged between my recently arrived dresser and the wall. I grab the book and climb into bed with it.

Chapter Five is called *Dark Ones: An Ongoing Problem*. It confirms what Marc said: that Dark Ones like to lure ordinary vampires into their sinister fold, and that Council members and their families are watched closely, to be sure they haven't gone over to the Dark side. I also learn that Dark Ones don't plan out their attacks in advance: They strike whoever happens to cross their path when they're hungry. Humans who might already be bleeding are especially vulnerable to attack.

Dark Ones do not kill their victims or turn them into vampires, I read as I slide down under the covers, shivering. *But their fangs release a poison that leaves those who are attacked in a frozen stupor. It usually takes the victims several days to fully recover.*

I think of Paige, lying in the local hospital. According to the whispers swirling around that afternoon, the substitute nurse decided to send her there. I wonder if she's come out of her stupor yet. Has she made the connection between her attack and Mr. Bernal's? Or maybe Carmen and Wendy — who no doubt have stopped by with flowers and candy — told her their theories about me. I wonder if a doctor or nurse on call noticed the similarity between Paige's wounds and those of the surfer.

And I know it's less important than catching the Dark Ones, but I can't help wondering how Paige's absence will affect the play.

The next day, at rehearsal, I get my answer.

Mr. Harker asks the cast and crew to gather around. We all oblige, everyone's face taut with worry. (Except for Gordon's; he's probably thinking about programming.) I'm careful not to make eye contact with Sasha or Marc. Whenever I saw Marc today, I was tempted to tell him that I found my Handbook or ask him if he had any new thoughts on the attacks. But then I'd remind myself of my popularity goal, and I'd glance away.

As far as I can tell, Marc has kept his promise: Sasha hasn't said anything to me. I suspect she — like many of my other classmates — thinks I'm so traumatized from finding Paige that I don't want to talk much, period.

"As you know," Mr. Harker begins solemnly, "Paige Olsen suffered a terrible accident on Tuesday."

At this, Carmen bursts into tears and Wendy wraps her in a hug. I see Sasha rolling her eyes, and I resist the urge to do the same.

"According to her doctors," Mr. Harker continues, "it will take some time for Paige to heal. She will most likely be too weak to participate in the play."

Carmen lets out a sob. "Then we should cancel it!" she declares.

Mr. Harker gives her a cutting look. "We will do no such thing," he tells her. "As I well remember from my childhood days as an actor," he adds, a note of pride creeping into his voice, "the familiar expression was, 'the show must go on.' And it must. Principal Anderson even feels the play will boost the morale of the student body."

Too bad the play's about vampires, I think. I hear Marc cough, and I'm positive he's sharing that thought.

"Unfortunately, we didn't cast understudies," Mr. Harker says. "So we need someone to step up and fill Paige's role. Someone who can learn her lines quickly and, ideally, looks the part. . . ." His eyes drift over to me, and my whole body tenses up.

No, no, no. Anyone but me. Carmen and Wendy are practically baring their teeth at me, silently daring me to volunteer myself. Sweat breaks out on my forehead. *Why* did I critique Paige at that rehearsal? Why couldn't Sasha have said something, too? She hadn't been a fan of Paige's performance. *"I just want to speak her lines* for *her,"* she had whispered to me.

Wait.

That's it!

I excitedly lift my hand, and Carmen and Wendy gasp.

"Yes, Ashlee?" Mr. Harker says.

"I'd like to nominate Sasha Hirsh for the role," I announce.

More gasps from the crowd.

Mr. Harker raises one eyebrow, clearly intrigued.

"She knows all the lines," I explain, and glance over at Sasha, who is staring at me, openmouthed. "She has a loud — well, good voice for the stage. She may not look like Vera in the movie, but that doesn't matter. She's — she's really pretty," I add haltingly. But it's true. In a way, Sasha's crazy fashion sense, combined with her looks, makes her much more unique and interesting than . . . well, than Paige.

Carmen and Wendy gawk at me. Marc grins and shakes his head. And Sasha looks the most stunned of all. I can understand. I haven't been exactly friendly to her. Of course, I'm only suggesting that she play Vera to save my own skin. But it's a little rewarding to see her eyes start to shine.

"You make a convincing case, Ashlee," says Mr. Harker. "I'd be all for it, but Sasha is indispensable as our stage manager. Who can fill in for her?"

Now it's my turn to gawk when Wendy speaks up.

"I can," she says. "Being prop master isn't all that demanding, so I have extra time. Sasha can explain the basics to me. All I need is the headset, right?" She looks sort of psyched at the prospect of getting to boss people around. Carmen blinks at her friend, clearly unsettled by this turn of events.

"Well, Sasha?" Mr. Harker asks. Everyone turns to see her response.

For the first time since I've known her, Sasha seems at a loss for words. She bites her lip and tugs on a stray curl.

"Um . . . I *could* give Wendy a crash course in stage-managing," she says, her voice uncharacteristically soft. "And, uh, I guess I do have all the lines memorized, because I'm always checking the script. I've never acted before, but . . ."

"Oh, just do it, Sasha!" Gordon says, surprising everyone. I'd had no idea he was even listening.

A smile creeps across Sasha's face. "Okay," she says. She throws up her hands, bracelets clanking. "For as long as Paige can't do it, I'll play Vera."

Marc gives his twin a fist bump, and even Wendy looks pleased. I'm surprised to feel a burst of gladness. It's not that I'm happy Paige is out of the picture. But it's hard to deny that Sasha will be a much better Vera.

"Woot!" James shouts, pumping a fist in the air. "Uh, I hope Paige gets better real soon, though," he adds, looking away from Carmen's glare.

"Excellent," Mr. Harker says, clapping his hands. "Okay, gang. Before we start rehearsing, the whole cast needs to go backstage with Ashlee for your fittings."

I nod but feel a twinge of terror. I'll be going back to where I discovered Paige. The whole cast turns pale, so I know they're thinking the same thing.

If Mr. Harker notices our hesitation, he doesn't address it. "Tomorrow morning," he continues, "I'll bring the costumes to be tailored at the dry cleaners. But since some of the alterations might take a while, we won't be able to hold a dress rehearsal." A groan goes up among the cast. "I know, I know," he says. "But we'll have a quick run-through during lunch on Friday."

The cast and crew break up, buzzing about Paige and Sasha. Meanwhile, I take a deep breath. What if there's another body sprawled on the floor of the costume room? I wish I knew where Dark Ones were lingering, and when they planned to strike next. *Marc was right*, I realize. *We need to do something before there's another attack.*

I'm making myself walk up the steps to the stage when Sasha appears beside me.

"Hey," she says, giving me a cautious smile. "Thanks. For suggesting me. I wouldn't have expected that."

"Well . . ." I shrug, feeling embarrassed. "You were the obvious choice. And," I add, looking down at my patterned tights, "I owed you one . . . for, you know, saving my life and all. In the bathroom?" It occurs to me then that I could tell Sasha the story behind my accident that day. She knows about bat-shifting. She would understand.

Sasha laughs as we go backstage. "I don't think I technically saved your life, Ashlee. But sure, I suppose we're even now." As I nervously open the door to the costume room, she adds, "I bet you picked out some awesome dresses for Vera."

"Oh — thanks," I say, flattered.

It's the strangest thing, but with Sasha next to me, I'm not scared in the costume room. I realize something: Sasha may not be popular, but she's . . . pleasant. Nice to be around.

Maybe I'm being ridiculous, avoiding her and Marc. I need to talk to *someone* about the Dark Ones, especially now that Arabella's not getting back to me. I know Marc would be helpful, and if Sasha gets involved — that wouldn't be the worst thing in the world. Maybe I should take Marc up on his invitation from yesterday.

Maybe.

Chapter Ten

The next afternoon, fate — or, rather, Mr. Harker — makes the decision for me. I'm standing at my locker at the end of the day, and he jogs up to me, out of breath and carrying a bulky garment bag.

"Ashlee," he says, looking stressed, "can you do me a huge favor? I just picked up Vera's costumes from the tailor, but I have a doctor's appointment. Would you be able to give the dresses directly to Sasha now? I want to be sure she has time to try them on, in case there need to be last-minute fixes before the show."

"Um, sure," I say, knowing that, as wardrobe master, I can't say no.

Mr. Harker thanks me, hands me the garment bag, and hurries off.

I glance around the empty hallway, past the crimson-bright *At First Bite* posters on the walls. I drank a Sanga! in the library before coming to my locker, so it's on the late side. Sasha's probably left already, which means I'll have to bring the costumes to her house.

I feel a mix of excitement and nervousness. I've wanted to talk to her and Marc all day but never had a chance. So I gather my courage and shut my locker.

I memorized Marc's address from the directory, and it's not a long walk from school. When I arrive at the house, though, I gasp. It's a full-on mansion, wide and majestic, with a blue pool glistening behind it. I would have *never* guessed that Marc and Sasha were so wealthy. I suddenly feel even more nervous, especially since I'm showing up unannounced.

I hug the garment bag to my chest and ring the bell. A beautiful African-American woman about my mom's age opens the door. She gives me a warm smile and I immediately see the resemblance between her and Sasha. And Marc has her big, long-lashed brown eyes. She's clearly their mom.

You're a vampire! I want to tell her. *On the Council!* But I struggle to keep the words from leaping off my tongue.

"Hi, I'm Ashlee Lambert," I say instead. "I'm here to give Sasha her —"

"Her costumes, yes," the woman says, opening the door all the way. "I've heard all about you, Ashlee. Please come in. I'm Mrs. Hirsh."

I wonder what Marc and Sasha — but mainly Marc — told their mother about me.

I take off my sun hat (I've been good about wearing it outside) and step inside. The house is full of fancy furniture and fine art, but it also feels cozy and welcoming.

"Sasha! Honey?" Mrs. Hirsh calls, peering up the grand staircase. She shrugs. "Maybe she's in here with her dad," she adds, leading me into the living room.

The first thing I spot is a shiny gold statuette on the mantel: It's an *Oscar*! Who *are* these people? Then I see the man sitting on the sofa, reading from an iPad.

"Sasha and Marc are both upstairs," he says, looking up with a smile.

He has blond-gray hair and Sasha's hazel eyes, and I realize that I *know* him. He's Ben Hirsh, the totally famous, Oscar-winning actor! So *that* was why I'd thought Sasha's last name had sounded familiar when I'd heard it my first day at S.M.A.

I'm speechless. I've never met a real movie star before, and I never expected to find one at Sasha and Marc's house. I probably should tell him I'm a big fan, but I've never seen his movies (they're mostly, like, boring political dramas). Plus, all I *want* to say is: *You're famous and you live with two vampires!*

"Ben, this is Ashlee," Mrs. Hirsh explains, resting one hand on my shoulder. Her fingers are ice-cold, but, funnily enough, I feel a sudden warmth. The warmth of recognition. "She's recently moved here from New York, and she's working on the play with Marc and Sasha."

"Ah, *At First Bite*?" Ben Hirsh grins, the corners of his eyes crinkling up. "I still can't get over the fact that Marc is involved in a play about vampires. I mean, talk about hitting close to ho —"

Mrs. Hirsh stops him short with an intense, *what-are-you-thinking?* look. It's clear that neither of them know that I'm a vampire. I'm grateful to Marc for keeping my secret, but at the same time something else is stirring inside me. I'm not sure if it's because I'm feeling starstruck, or safe, or both. All I know is I'm tired of hiding and scrambling and living in fear. And I can't stop myself from blurting out the truth.

"No, I get it," I say, my face burning. "You see, the play hits close to home for me, too. I'm —" I look at Mrs. Hirsh. "I'm one of you."

Stunned silence fills the room, and then a voice calls out:

"Wait, *what*? You're a vampire?"

I turn and see Sasha standing at the entrance to the living room, her eyes enormous. Marc is right behind her, a sheepish expression on his face.

"I am," I say, trembling a little. It's the first time I've admitted it out loud, and it feels surprisingly good.

Then everyone starts talking at once.

"I don't believe it!" Mr. Hirsh says, jumping to his feet. "What are the chances?"

"Really? Who's your mentor?" Mrs. Hirsh asks me, surprise etched on her face.

"Arabella Lowe," I tell her. Then I add, "At least, I hope she still is. I haven't heard from her in a while."

"But — but there were no signs," Sasha sputters, staring at me. "Nothing to give you away."

"Well, that time you found me in the bathroom," I explain, my heart pounding as I grip the garment bag. "I fell because I was having issues with my bat-shifting."

"Oh, poor dear," Mrs. Hirsh murmurs, frowning. "Bat-shifting can take some getting used to."

The only person not talking is Marc, and Sasha suddenly notices.

"You *knew* this, didn't you?" Sasha cries, spinning around to glare at her brother. "And you told her — about you? About Mom? And you never told us?"

Marc holds up his hands as if to shield himself. "Look, it just sort of happened," he replies. "Ashlee saw me drinking Sanga!, and we got to talking about Dark Ones. . . ."

"It's true," I say quickly, coming to his defense. "I thought Marc was the Dark One who'd been attacking people in our school. Then he explained to me about your mom" — I glance quickly at Mrs. Hirsh — "being on the Council."

"I wish you'd told me you'd met another vampire at school," Mrs. Hirsh says to Marc, shaking her head.

"Yes, son," Mr. Hirsh chimes in. "Especially since you know your mother and the other Council members have been so focused on the attacks."

"Plus, I thought we told each other everything," Sasha harrumphs.

Marc shrugs, and his brown eyes meet mine. "I promised Ashlee I'd keep her secret," he says simply.

His cheeks turn a little red, and I smile at him, blushing, too.

"Actually," I say, biting my lip. "I came here in part hoping we could talk more about the attacks. I don't have any new leads, but I'm worried something else is going to happen soon." I look uncertainly from Marc to his mother.

Mrs. Hirsh glances at her watch. "Unfortunately, Dad and I have dinner at Steven Spielberg's tonight," she says, in the same way someone might say they had to pick up groceries. "But, Ashlee," she adds, "feel free to stay as long as you like. Marc can fill me in later on what you discuss." She shoots Marc a stern *won't-you?* look, and he nods.

"You guys go on upstairs," Mr. Hirsh says. "Mom and I have to get ready, and George Clooney will be here any minute to pick us up."

Maybe you can get used to being a vampire, but how do you ever get used to hearing *that*?

Ten minutes later, Marc, Sasha, and I are ensconced in Sasha's bedroom. It's as crazily decorated as I would imagine: leopard-print rug, multicolored scarves instead of curtains, and posters of indie bands I've never heard of on the walls. Marc is sitting in Sasha's neon orange desk chair, looking on her computer, and I'm sitting cross-legged on her bed, sipping a Sanga! that Marc brought up from the kitchen. Sasha has just emerged from her private bathroom in Vera's green gown.

She looks amazing. The dress fits perfectly now and the color makes her skin tone glow. I want to tell her as much, but she's clearly focused on other matters. She plops down beside me on the bed (I cringe, hoping she won't wrinkle the skirt) and says firmly, "All right, you guys. Tell me *everything*."

I'm still not quite able to believe that Sasha knows my secret now. That her whole family does. But it also feels like a heavy weight has been lifted from my chest.

"I've told you from the get-go, sis," Marc says, reaching for his own Sanga! "I think there's a Dark One in our school who's behind the attacks."

"Same here," I say, "I read in the Vampire's Handbook" — I look pointedly at Marc when I say this — "that Dark Ones only attack people who happen to cross their path when they're hungry. So it doesn't make sense that someone from the outside would come into our school just to find fresh blood."

"So who have you suspected so far?" Sasha asks

me, and grins wickedly. "I mean, besides my blood-thirsty brother."

I chuckle, relieved that Sasha's no longer sullen. "Nurse Murray was at the top of my list," I confess, "since she's new to the school and was the one to find Mr. Bernal."

Sasha gives me a thoughtful look. "Sounds like the same reason Carmen and Wendy gave for blaming *you* for what happened to Paige," she says gently.

"I know." I shift uncomfortably on the bed. "But I don't think Nurse Murray's guilty anymore. She wasn't even in school the day Paige was attacked."

"We can't discount anyone, though," Marc points out. "I've considered Nurse Murray, too. I've even wondered about Ms. Anderson."

"Hang on. That's not a bad idea!" I say excitedly. I can sort of picture our principal, with her ramrod-straight posture and neat gray bob, bat-shifting. "Remember how snippy and bossy she was when Mr. Bernal was discovered?" I add. "She seemed very eager to ship him off to the hospital."

"Uh-huh," Marc says, clicking away on his computer. "She could have been the one to recommend sending Paige to the hospital, too. Just to hush up the victims."

"But why do you assume it's an adult?" Sasha asks. "It could be any student over age twelve." She looks at me, shrugging. "After all, I had no clue *you* were a vampire until today. Someone else could be hiding in plain sight."

"Exactly," I say, my thoughts whirring. "The possibilities are endless. But I think that if anyone can crack this case, it's us." I look from Sasha to Marc, knowing it to be true. There's an energy in the room, a sense that the three of us work well together.

"Here's what I don't get, though," Sasha says, tucking her legs up under her (I cringe again — the dress!). "Obviously, *we've* all thought of it, but why has no one else made the connection between these attacks and vampires?"

"They're getting there," Marc says, his eyes glued to the computer. "Come here and look at this article in the *Santa Monica Daily Press*," he adds, motioning for us to join him. We do, leaning over to see the screen.

VAMPIRE FEVER?

Paige Olsen, a local twelve-year-old girl, was admitted to St. John's Hospital on Tuesday, displaying neck wounds very similar to those of the twenty-year-old surfer discovered on Santa Monica Beach on Saturday. The doctor on call, Dr. Cullen Meyer, reported that the wounds also matched those of a sixty-three-year-old school custodian who was admitted last week. The doctor and other experts have begun speculating that the series of attacks might have something to do with the recent pop culture craze surrounding vampires.

"Tests are being run," Dr. Meyer stated, "but the wounds look as if they were made by fangs. For all we know, some lunatic is out there, wearing fake fangs and thinking it's a great idea to try to suck people's blood."

Indeed, there is a ravenous appetite for all things vampire. Santa Monica Academy, where Ms. Olsen is a student, and where the custodian is employed, is staging a production of the classic vampire movie *At First Bite*. Some experts are wondering: Is our obsession with bloodsuckers becoming dangerous?

"Whoa," Marc says, sitting back against the chair. "I wonder if anyone from school has seen this. Do you think they'll try to call off the play?"

"I hope not," I say, my stomach churning. "Plays and movies and books shouldn't be blamed just because these Dark vampires are determined to do evil things."

"That could be it, though," Sasha says, tapping her bottom lip. "The *play*."

"What do you mean?" Marc and I ask at the same time, then grin at each other before facing Sasha again.

"I think someone who's involved in the play must have been the one to attack Paige," Sasha explains, beginning to pace back and forth. "After all, Ashlee, you just said that Dark Ones only attack whoever's right in front of them. So someone must have already been backstage when Paige got there on Tuesday. Then, after biting her, they bolted."

"You're right," I say, cold dread filling my belly. My mind races through the cast and crew, and then pauses on the impossible. "Do you think it could be — Carmen? Or Wendy? Maybe Carmen was acting so upset as a cover-up. Or maybe Wendy was blaming me to get the attention off herself." I think back to the initiation ceremony in New York. Just as I hadn't noticed Marc, I could have just as easily overlooked one of those girls.

"Well, they certainly are evil," Sasha mutters, and I decide not to argue with her. Now's not the time. "But if they were vampires, Marc would have recognized them at the initiation ceremony, right?" she adds, echoing my thoughts.

Marc shrugs. "It was so dark in that room, and I was freaked out." I nod at him, remembering that night. "Someone from our school *could* have been there," he reasons.

Sasha bites her lip, looking hesitantly at her brother. "So maybe it's someone we'd never imagine. Like . . ." She drops her voice to a whisper. "Gordon."

"No way." Marc shakes his head emphatically. "Gordon would *not* be slick enough to hide the fact that he's a vampire, let alone a Dark One." He pauses. "How about James Okada? He's friends with Paige's crowd, but he obviously isn't too bummed that Paige isn't playing Vera anymore. Maybe he even *wanted* her out of the show?"

"Well, can you blame him?" I say, then feel a flash of guilt. "I mean, um, she wasn't very good."

Sasha and Marc laugh, and I realize there's no point in pretending about Paige anymore. "She was *terrible*." Sasha sighs. "Not that I'm sure I'll be much better. . . ."

"You will be," Marc assures his sister, and she gives him a grateful smile.

"I can't believe Mr. Harker allowed her to be cast as the lead," I muse out loud as I sit back down on the bed. "He's such a perfectionist about everything else."

Sasha nods. "It's because he was out sick during the casting, and the teacher filling in for him didn't care who got cast. Paige basically just demanded the role."

A small bell is ringing in my head. "Mr. Harker was sick?" I ask.

Marc looks at me, his eyes growing wide.

"Yeah," Sasha says. "He was sick a lot during the first semester. The flu and stuff. That's why he never got around to casting understudies either."

"Oh my God," I whisper. I jump up again, my heart pounding. "That's it, you guys! That's it!"

"What's it?" Sasha asks.

Marc stands up, nodding at me. "I can't believe it never occurred to me before."

Everything is clicking together. I remember how cold Mr. Harker's hands were when he moved me aside in the costume room. I'd figured he was nervous. But no.

"He was a child actor, right?" I say, motioning to the computer. "I bet if we checked online, we'd see that he stopped acting around the age of twelve. . . ."

"When he could no longer show up on film," Marc finishes for me, sitting back down and clicking over to IMDB.

"Hang on," Sasha says, looking from me to Marc. "Are you saying Mr. Harker is a vampire? That *he's* the Dark One?"

It's difficult for me to grasp the idea, too. I've always liked Mr. Harker. I can't imagine him hurting people. But there's no getting around it.

"He has to be," Marc says, glancing back at me and Sasha. "Dark Ones get sick if they go too long without human blood. Mr. Harker probably got recruited by some local Dark Ones, back in the fall. Maybe he resisted attacking humans at first, and that's why he kept getting sick. But now he's never sick at all. Not since we got back from break and Mr. Bernal was attacked."

"And it wasn't Ms. Anderson who said that Mr. Bernal should be taken away," I gasp, remembering. "It was Mr. Harker. *He* hinted to Ms. Anderson that Mr. Bernal was crazy."

"What about the surfer?" Sasha asks, looking a bit skeptical. "Was Mr. Harker behind that attack, too?"

"I'm not sure," I say, reaching into my bag and taking out my cell phone. "But I have to text my mentor and tell her we solved the mystery."

"Yeah, I should call Mom," Marc says, pulling his own phone out of his jeans pocket. "Maybe we can have the Council go to Mr. Harker's house right now —"

"Guys, wait!" Sasha exclaims, and Marc and I lower our phones. "This is *all* just based on our speculation. We're going to need actual proof if we want to accuse Mr. Harker of these horrible crimes."

"Well, how are we going to get proof?" I ask, feeling helpless. "None of the victims saw him — just a bat."

Marc looks at me and Sasha, his jaw set in that determined way. "Then we have no choice, do we?" he says. "We'll have to set a trap."

Chapter Eleven

The next day, I feel more like a zombie than a vampire. I stayed at Sasha and Marc's house until late, going over the plan. We filled in Mrs. Hirsh when she got home, but it took a lot of convincing to get her to agree to it. When *I* got home, I sent an epic e-mail to Arabella, telling her everything. So I only slept a few hours.

In homeroom, Mr. Harker looks as tense and tired as I feel, which is a good thing: He doesn't seem to notice how Sasha and I recoil every time he glances at us. I wonder if being a Dark One is taking a toll on him — or if he's just preoccupied with the play.

The play seems to be on everyone's mind. As I walk the halls, I spot kids tearing down *At First Bite* posters and talking about "bad influences" and "vampire wannabes." Clearly, word has spread beyond the online article.

I now get the need for vampires' secrecy: If people knew what was *really* going on, there'd be mass hysteria.

At our lunchtime run-through in the auditorium, Mr. Harker makes an announcement. "As you may have heard," he says, "there's been some recent, uh, controversy about our play's subject matter." He clears his throat, and Sasha, Marc, and I exchange meaningful glances. "But please know that the show *will* go on."

This time, the three of us exchange relieved glances. We need the show to go on; otherwise, our plan is useless.

"Good!" Carmen pipes up. "Because guess who might be making a guest appearance in the audience tonight?" She pauses dramatically, then squeals, *"Paige!"*

"She was released from the hospital earlier than expected!" Wendy chimes in.

I see Sasha swallow hard, and I know she's not thinking about our scheme right now. Paige will be watching Sasha's performance like a hawk, ready to pounce on any mistake. The same goes for the costumes, of course.

As if we needed more stuff to worry about tonight.

While the cast runs through their lines, the crew goes backstage to set things up. I quickly prepare everyone's costumes for each scene, and then I take care of *other* business. I drag the headless mannequin down the narrow hallway, positioning it near the prop closet. I drape Vera's lace apron over it and stick a few pins in its body. Marc, watching from the control booth, gives me the thumbs-up sign. We're ready.

The rest of the afternoon passes in a blur. When the final bell rings, I head for the auditorium, racked with nerves. Out of habit, I text Eve and Mallory:

Opening night in a few minutes! Wish me luck!

I realize with a smile that I'm finally not lying to my friends about my extracurricular activities. But I am leaving out a big part of what else is going to happen tonight.

The air backstage is crackling with nerves and excitement. Wendy is barking orders into her headset microphone, Gordon is climbing the ladder to the control booth, and Mr. Harker is checking the set decorations onstage. I'm relieved he's out of earshot.

I feel a huge thrill when I see some of the cast members bustling around — in costume! They look terrific: James is dapper and dashing in his dark suit, and Carmen is elegant in the purple dress I picked out for Mila's first scene. She even stops me as I walk past, putting a hand on my arm and saying, "Thanks, Ashlee. I love all of Mila's clothes."

Her expression is earnest, and I can tell that this is her way of apologizing for what happened in the costume room on Tuesday. She and Wendy haven't spoken to me since then, but they haven't been overtly cruel either. Maybe I'm back on track with them. I'm happy, but I have to find Sasha, so I thank Carmen and hurry off.

I bump into Sasha coming out of the girls' dressing room. She looks stunning in Vera's white lace dress, with her curls piled up on her head. But her face is a chalky gray.

"Are you having second thoughts?" I ask, reaching out to squeeze her hand. It's a natural gesture, one I don't think twice about. A gesture you'd make toward a friend.

"No," she chokes out. "I mean —" She clears her throat. "I'm kind of freaked, yeah. But we *have* to do this. And it will be okay."

"It will," I tell her, thinking *I hope so.* "Sorry my hands are cold," I add. "Probably not too comforting, huh?"

She laughs. "Are you kidding? I live in a house of cold-handed people. It's actually very comforting."

I laugh, too, feeling some of my nervousness fade. Just then, Marc appears, looking calm and steady.

"Mom texted me," he whispers. "They're all arriving in the auditorium now."

At that moment, Mr. Harker ducks in from the stage. "The audience is starting to come in!" he calls. "Cast, take your places in the wings. Crew, please do any last-minute checks."

"This is it," Sasha murmurs, drawing in a big breath. I catch myself — and Marc — doing the same. The three of us look at each other, knowing we have to be brave.

"Good luck, guys," Marc says, giving Sasha a hug before she runs off to the wings. Then he turns to me and gives my hand a quick squeeze — cold on cold. For some reason, this friendly gesture makes my cheeks get very hot. He grins at me before bounding up the ladder to the control booth.

I step toward the curtain. I know I should be making sure no one's shoes are scuffed or buttons are missing. But I can't resist — I tug aside the heavy velvet and peer out into the crowd.

My stomach leaps. Despite (or maybe because of) all the protests and controversy, the auditorium is *packed*. Every seat is filled, and people are chattering in anticipation. The production assistants are passing out glossy programs, and I feel a burst of pride, knowing my name is listed in them under "Wardrobe Master."

I squint, wondering who's out there. Mom? Paige? Some big-shot agents?

But then Gordon dims the lights, Marc starts up the spooky music, and a hush falls over the crowd.

Showtime.

I scurry away from the curtain, heading to my post outside the costume room.

From there, I hear the play beginning. Sasha, her voice carrying beautifully, says, "The year was 1789 . . ." and I can picture her, standing beneath the lone spotlight. Right away I know she's going to be awesome. I guess she inherited her dad's acting genes.

I look around. Mr. Harker is watching the play from the wings. Wendy is outside the prop closet, eyeing Marc and Gordon in the booth. Everything is in place.

Then I hear it: our cue. Sasha says, loudly: "The guests for the ball will be arriving soon, and I must retire to bed."

The music is supposed to boom dramatically, but Marc — as planned — presses a button and a Rihanna song blares out.

I hear the audience laugh nervously. Mr. Harker balls his hands into fists, looking furious. Wendy, as we knew she would, storms toward the control booth and hisses up to Marc, "*What* did you just do?"

Marc is already clambering down the ladder. I hear him whisper to Wendy, "Sorry — I'm not feeling well — can you take over for a sec?"

There's no way Wendy can refuse, not when her reputation as a flawless stage manager is at stake. She grudgingly agrees and asks me if I can handle any prop issues in the meantime. I nod and watch as she climbs up the ladder in her UGGs. She sits down beside Gordon and puts on the giant earphones. Neither of them will be able to hear anything that goes on backstage.

So far, so good.

Marc nods at me, and he runs off toward the stage-left wings. There, he and Sasha explained to me last night, is a small secret door that allows people to enter undetected from the auditorium. That's where Marc will be meeting his mom and the two other Council members. Hopefully, the audience won't notice a few people — vampires — sneaking backstage.

"Good night then, Vladimir!" I hear Sasha say. It's time for her to walk offstage and time for Vladimir and the rest of the cast to start the ballroom scene.

I watch as Sasha appears in the wings, flushed and glowing.

"You're doing great," Mr. Harker tells her, but he sounds tense.

"The music mistake threw me off," Sasha whispers as we'd planned. "Can you talk me through my next scene? I just have to grab my apron off the mannequin."

"Of course," Mr. Harker says, and together they walk away from the wings. I step back and disappear into the shadows, grateful for the all-black outfit every crew member has to wear.

"Where's Ashlee?" Mr. Harker hisses, looking around. "And where is that ridiculous mannequin?"

"It's here," Sasha says, leading him down the narrow hallway. She stops in front of the mannequin. Then, as we rehearsed it last night, she reaches out a finger and pricks it on one of the pins.

"Ouch!" she whisper-cries. As Mr. Harker and I look on, a ruby red drop of blood seeps to the surface of her skin.

Nothing happens at first, and I feel like I can't breathe.

What if we judged Mr. Harker wrong? What if Sasha pricked her finger for nothing? What if we're not going to catch the Dark One tonight after all?

And then, in a heartbeat, Mr. Harker begins shifting.

His shifting is fast, and focused. Razor-sharp fangs dart out of his mouth. Long, leathery wings unfold from his shrinking body His eyes glow dark red. He is no longer Mr. Harker, kindly English teacher and play director. He is a merciless, hungry vampire bat.

Sasha doesn't scream — she's seen bat-shifting many times before. But then the bat lunges at her and she stumbles back, ducking behind the mannequin.

A horrified shriek builds in my throat. *He's still going to get her — we shouldn't have put her in danger — where are the others?* By now, Marc and the Council members should have arrived. What if something went wrong and they don't show up?

Suddenly, I know what I have to do.

I step out from the shadows. "Mr. Harker!" I say.

The bat jerks around. Clearly stunned to see me, he immediately shifts back, becoming a young teacher in jeans once more. Sasha leans against the wall behind the mannequin, breathing rapidly and holding her finger.

I frown at Mr. Harker. "You're a Dark One!" I whisper, all my shock and anger bubbling to the surface.

To my surprise, Mr. Harker blinks at me calmly. "And you're a vampire, Ashlee," he says. "I knew it. I knew it when I saw your reaction to living in Vladimir's castle that first day in homeroom. And when your eyes turned red as you were shifting. I was glad when you signed up for the play. I even wondered if, over time, I could become like a second mentor to you."

"Never," I retort in disgust. "I'd never want to be like you —"

"But being a Dark One is natural," he says silkily, and I realize this is how Dark Ones recruit their members. "Vampires are meant to feast upon human blood. Not trifle with small wild creatures, or worse, that Sanga! abomination." He shudders.

"Sanga! is delicious," I hiss, offended.

Mr. Harker stares longingly at Sasha's bloody fingertip. I want to tell her to run. But before I can, Mr. Harker's eyes turn red again and fangs creep out of the corners of his mouth. Within an instant, he's bat-shifted once more. This time, the bat zips around the mannequin, shooting straight for Sasha's neck.

Sasha's eyes are huge with fear and she's holding out her arms, as if that could stop him.

But I can.

I concentrate with all my might. *You can do this, Ashlee.* I visualize the wings sprouting from my body, my ears growing long and pointy. I remind myself of how I shifted back behind the palm tree. *You can do this.*

And I do. I bat-shift.

By now, the Dark bat has Sasha cornered, and his fangs are mere inches from her throat. So I zoom forward, flapping my wings hard, and drive myself between them. For a second, Mr. Harker and I face off, two bats hovering in the narrow hallway while Sasha cowers and the music soars onstage.

Then, mercifully, I hear footsteps. Voices. People are running from the stage-left wings. I spin around in midair and see Marc. He's leading five determined-looking vampires, including his mother, and . . .

Arabella!

It's really my mentor, here in Los Angeles, her red curls flying behind her as she races toward us. I'm so happy to see her that I instantly start shifting back.

"You there! Dark One!" one of the Council members — a tall, bearded, and imposing man — booms in a deep voice. "We are from the Los Angeles Vampire Council. Shift back immediately."

I look over to see Mr. Harker obeying. His wings lengthen into arms and his feet hit the dusty floor.

"Nothing — nothing happened," he stammers, lifting up his hands as the crowd closes in around him. "I'm innocent."

"We *saw* you," hisses Mrs. Hirsh. "You were about to attack *my daughter*." She grabs a trembling Sasha and pulls her into a fierce hug.

I want to run over and hug Arabella, but I'm frozen with fear and uncertainty.

Sasha looks much calmer now. She hugs her mom back, then dabs at her fingertip, checking to make sure the bleeding has stopped. Then she says, "Mom,

I'm okay. Promise. I need to go back onstage." Glaring at Mr. Harker, she grabs Vera's apron off the trusty mannequin and runs to the wings.

Never once did I doubt that Sasha would be the right girl for the job. Mrs. Hirsh was concerned, of course, but Marc and I had both insisted that she was tough enough — and familiar enough with vampires — to step up to the task. Sasha had agreed.

A moment later, I hear her speaking her lines onstage like a true professional. I wonder if the audience has any clue about the drama unfolding backstage.

"We have five vampire witnesses, Dark One," the bearded man is saying. He steps close to Mr. Harker, whose face pales. "You cannot lie to us. Confess."

"Actually, make that seven vampire witnesses," Arabella says, glancing from Marc to me. She grins at me and I grin back. I notice then that there's a handsome guy about her age standing next to her — it's her boyfriend, Beau!

"You're a vampire?" Mr. Harker asks Marc, looking startled, and Marc nods proudly.

Mr. Harker sways on his feet, sweat beading on his forehead. "I — I — please forgive me, Council. I was led astray. Other Dark Ones in the region made me into one of them. I never intended to attack so often, and I certainly never wanted to harm children."

"But you did," Marc speaks up, his eyes fiery. "You attacked Paige, didn't you? And Mr. Bernal, too."

Mr. Harker nods, looking close to tears. I can't tell if he's truly remorseful or just a very good actor. "As well as the young surfer on the beach," he mumbles. "My hunger was too great."

"Sorry to hear that," snaps another Council member, a brunette woman about my mom's age who looks capable of knocking Mr. Harker out cold. "You can tell us more about your actions, and those of your friends, when we leave here." She steps forward menacingly.

"How are we going to do this?" Arabella asks Mrs. Hirsh. "People will notice the director being escorted out in the middle of the play."

She's right. Especially since the ball scene has ended, and cast members are starting to crowd into the wings. They don't see what's going on down the hallway right now, but they might soon.

Wait.

The ball scene has ended. Suddenly, I realize what part of the play we're up to — the bat puppets are supposed to fly out onstage.

I glance up at the control booth. Wendy is otherwise occupied, so she'll have no idea that we won't use the prop bats.

Quickly, I whisper my plan to everyone.

"Excellent idea," Mrs. Hirsh whispers. "Marc, you'll have to join us," she adds. "We'll need backup. Ashlee, you stay here."

Then they all start bat-shifting, one by one: Arabella, the bearded guy, the brunette woman, Beau, and Mrs. Hirsh. Then Marc — I'm impressed by how well he does it. Mr. Harker shifts as well — he has no choice — but this time he looks defeated, not vicious.

Listening to the play, I give the signal, and they all fly forward. I race after them, watching from the stage-left wings as they swoop out onto the stage in a big black mass. Sasha really does look like she wants to faint, so it's probably easy for her to scream and swoon backward. The audience bursts into applause, no doubt impressed by how realistic the bats look.

But the audience doesn't seem to notice how one of the bats is hemmed in — sandwiched between the two biggest and burliest bats. They also don't seem to mind that the bats soar over their heads and out of the auditorium. I know that they will then fly out into the night. I also know, from what Mrs. Hirsh told us yesterday, that they will bring Mr. Harker to the Vampire Disciplinary Committee, where he will be dealt with properly.

I let out a big breath. I back out of the wings and run into James and Carmen. They're asking me where Mr. Harker is and exclaiming over how great the bats looked, but I'm too exhausted to answer. I know I should be manning the costume room, but for a minute, I need a little break.

So when no one's looking, I hurry down the narrow hallway, past the mannequin, and into the prop closet. I shut the door and look around. There, hidden behind some wooden stools and the bag of bat puppets, is Marc's Sanga! cooler. I open it, grab a frosty container, and take a long, relieved sip.

I think I've earned it.

Chapter Twelve

When the play is over, the audience gives the cast a standing ovation. As I watch from the wings, I feel like they're cheering for me, Sasha, Marc, and all the vampires who came to the rescue.

But I can't relax completely: Marc hasn't returned yet, and I hope everything went okay.

The audience is still whistling and clapping when Ms. Anderson joins the cast onstage.

"I'm not sure where the esteemed director, Mr. Harker, is," she says, glancing into the wings, "but I'd like to thank him, and the wonderful cast and crew, for a stellar performance. I suppose vampires can be fun after all!" I smile wryly as more cheers erupt from the crowd. "I'd also like to invite everyone to the cafeteria for some celebratory cookies and punch," Ms. Anderson adds.

The cast streams into the wings, beaming, hugging, and congratulating each other. I immediately run up to Sasha and give her a huge hug.

"We did it, right?" she whispers, hugging me back. "It looked like the bats were carting him off."

I nod, frowning. "But I'm worried," I whisper. "Wouldn't Marc come back here? Or your mom? Do you think something went wrong?"

Sasha shakes her head. "They'll be at the party," she says confidently. "Marc wouldn't miss an opportunity for cookies. Come on," she adds, hiking up her long green skirt. "I even know a shortcut."

It must be Sasha's twin intuition at work; when we arrive in the cafeteria, Marc and Mrs. Hirsh are standing by the cookie table, talking. They look totally calm, as if it's been any ordinary Friday night.

When they spot us, Mrs. Hirsh and Marc wrap Sasha in a three-person hug. Mrs. Hirsh embraces me as well, and Marc, looking embarrassed, gives me a fast fist bump.

"I'm so sorry I was late bringing the Council members backstage," he says. "The door to the auditorium was jammed and it took forever to get it open."

"It worked out fine," I tell him truthfully. After all, if the others hadn't been late, I wouldn't have had a chance to bat-shift successfully!

"I'm so glad you girls are okay!" Mrs. Hirsh cries. Luckily, the cafeteria's still empty so nobody thinks it's strange that she's saying this.

"Did everything go well on your end?" I ask.

Mrs. Hirsh nods grimly. "We delivered Mr. Harker to the Disciplinary Committee without incident. As soon as he got there, he started blabbing about the other Dark Ones in Los Angeles. Apparently, a group of them moved here from Arizona and recruited Mr. Harker back in October."

"Right around the time the play was being cast," Marc puts in.

"Yes," Mrs. Hirsh says. "You three were right — he didn't want to attack humans at first, but he kept getting sick. It's the curse of the Dark Ones. His buddies, as we suspected, were to blame for the attacks elsewhere in the region. But now that they've been identified, the Disciplinary Committee will nab them, too."

"So, what about Mr. Harker?" Sasha asks, looking a little sad. "I guess he's never coming back to school, right? I mean, I know he tried to drink my blood, but he was a good teacher, and a good director."

Marc rolls his eyes. "Oh, please. He was totally pretentious."

"We had Mr. Harker sign a statement," Mrs. Hirsh explains, "that he brought a pet bat into the school, and this bat was responsible for the attacks. It's the only way to explain the attacks to the school administration, and also to ensure that he is fired." She rubs Sasha's shoulder. "I'm sorry, sweetie. He may have been a good teacher, but if he was so easily swayed by the Dark Ones, I don't think he was a good person, deep down."

I remember when Arabella said I could never be a Dark One, because I was, as she put it, a "softy." I may not be a softy, but I think I'm starting to understand what she meant. As a vampire, I can use my powers for good, not evil.

I did that tonight, after all.

Then, as if I've conjured her with my thoughts, Arabella pops up beside me. I throw my arms around her, breathing in her crisp floral scent.

"I can't believe you came to LA," I say, pulling back to stare at her.

"Of *course* I came," Arabella says, patting my cheek with her be-ringed hand. "Ash, I'm so sorry that I wasn't getting back to you. I was out of town. When I saw your e-mail from last night, I immediately got in touch with the Council here." She nods to Mrs. Hirsh. "They already were aware of the situation, but I knew I had to fly out to see you. Beau decided to come, too."

She blows a kiss to Beau, who is standing at the punch table.

"I'm so glad," I tell her, feeling a lump form in my throat.

"And I'm so *proud*," Arabella tells me, her eyes shining. "Ashlee, I saw what you did. As we were all coming backstage, I saw you bat-shift! You were spectacular."

"I — I was?" I ask, my face getting warm.

Arabella nods. "I told you that you could do it," she says, giving me a wise look. "You guys were amazing, too," she tells Sasha and Marc, who beam.

More people are crowding into the cafeteria, and I glance over my shoulder to see who's here. When I spot a certain someone, I feel a bolt of surprise. I excuse myself, then make my way through the throng.

"Mom?" I say when I reach her. She turns to me, her face lighting up. "You weren't sure you'd have time to come!" I exclaim as she kisses my cheek. It's almost as crazy to see her here as it was to see Arabella.

"I decided to make the time," Mom replies. "Filming can wait for a night. Honey," she adds, taking my hand, "I know I told you to try to get onstage, but I think you're cut out for fashion design. The costumes you chose were amazing. *Perfect*."

I soak up her praise, but then I think about the word *perfect*. My mom likes everything to be perfect, and I thought I did, too. But nothing is ever *really* perfect. Take me, Ashlee Samantha Lambert: At first glance, I appear to be a put-together twelve-year-old girl. And, in some ways, I am. But I'm also a vampire who's still figuring lots of stuff out. I'm far from perfect. And maybe that's okay.

"Look who else made it," Mom says, waving. I turn and see Dylan loping over, with the beautiful high school girl at his side.

"Hey, Ash," Dylan greets me sheepishly, his mouth full of cookies. "This is, um, Diana Chen. My . . . g-girlfriend," he chokes, his face the color of my legendary sunburn.

Girlfriend? He must be joking. I look at Mom, who is smiling approvingly. Then I gape at Diana, expecting her to burst out laughing or throw up.

Instead, she shakes my hand, saying, "Great to meet you, Ashlee. You did an awesome job with the costumes!"

"Yeah, sis," Dylan says clumsily, clapping me on the shoulder. "Well played."

"Thanks, bro." I laugh in surprise. I realize Dylan and I are breaking my golden rule by interacting this way — and then I realize I don't care. It's nice to be standing here with my family, like Sasha and Marc are doing across the room. I'm not yet ready to tell Mom or Dylan the truth about myself, but maybe in time I will be. It's something to consider, at least.

"Oh my God!" a voice cries out. "You're Judge Julia! From *Justice with Judge Julia*!"

I don't even have to look to know that it's Nurse Murray. She's standing behind me, gawking at Mom.

"Oh, that's right," I say, remembering my deal with the nurse. "Mom, this is Nurse Murray. She'd love your autograph."

"Of course!" Mom says, glowing. She reaches into her purse for a pen and paper. "I'm thrilled to oblige." It's obvious she's loving her moment of celebrity.

"Thank you, Ashlee," Nurse Murray says, wide-eyed, and I can't believe I ever suspected her of anything. "You know," she tells Mom, "I just auditioned for a reality show myself. . . ."

They start chatting, and I glance across the room. Arabella, Beau, and Mrs. Hirsh are talking by the cookie table. Marc and Gordon are standing off to the side, and it looks like Marc is assuring Gordon that no, he's not deathly ill. I also see that Mr. Hirsh has arrived, presenting Sasha with a big bouquet of flowers. There's a literal line of people snaking toward him, waiting for *his* autograph (Principal Anderson, of all people, is at the head of it).

Sasha sees me watching and trots over, holding her bouquet. I meet her halfway.

"I overheard Ms. Anderson saying that she wants to take a cast and crew photo," Sasha murmurs. "Obviously, you and Marc will have to avoid that."

"Well, are the rest of the cast and crew even here?" I ask, craning my neck to survey the cafeteria. "I see Gordon, but what about Wendy and —"

"Did I hear my name?"

A grinning Wendy has appeared at my side. She's standing with Carmen and . . .

170

Paige.

Aside from the white bandage on her neck, Paige looks like her old self: perfectly made-up and dressed in a trendy outfit. I'm relieved to see her, but it's funny — I don't feel that old intimidation.

"Are you all recovered?" I ask her.

"Mostly. I'm a very fast healer," she replies haughtily. "I still have no idea what happened. But Ms. Anderson just said that Mr. Harker's pet bat probably bit me?"

"That's awful," I say, studiously avoiding looking at Sasha.

"I think they're going to fire him," Carmen says. "But then who'll direct the play?"

"Maybe Nurse Murray," I offer. "She's really into drama."

Paige runs her eyes over Sasha. "You were . . . good," she tells her reluctantly. "Really good." She pauses, smoothing out her lip gloss with her pinkie. "My doctor says I should take it easy for the next couple weeks, so I don't know if I'll be able to play Vera at all. But if anyone had to fill in for me, well, you're not a bad second choice."

"Gee thanks, Paige," Sasha says. She rolls her eyes, but she's smiling.

Now that Paige has set the tone, Carmen and Wendy clearly feel safe to speak up as well.

"Yeah, you were great, Sasha," Wendy says, looking impressed. "Apparently, some agents in the audience were even talking about you. And I didn't know your dad was Ben Hirsh!"

Sasha shrugs. "I don't advertise it."

"It makes sense that you're such a good actress, then!" Carmen pipes up. "BTW, I loved how you did the fainting scene — oh, um." She glances guiltily at Paige.

But Paige isn't paying attention to Carmen. Now she's studying me. "You know, Ashlee," she says, "at first I wasn't wild about your costume picks, but they looked pretty cool onstage. Almost like a fashion show." Carmen and Wendy nod emphatically, like puppets. "Maybe I misjudged you," Paige adds, putting special emphasis on each word.

My heart flips over. Paige smiles at me, and I get what she's saying. That she was wrong to write me off. That I'm really just like her and her friends.

Only . . .

Am I?

"Actually," Paige goes on, still smiling at me. "Carmen is hosting an after-after-party at her house tonight. Very small and exclusive. Would you want to come?" She shoots a glance at Sasha. "You, too," she adds as an afterthought.

"Please, Ash!" Carmen says, as if she's been calling me *Ash* all this time.

"You can't miss it," Wendy puts in. "It'll be the party of the year." She sounds like Eve.

I feel a burst of victory. *It happened!* It happened exactly as I'd wanted it to. Finally, after all my hard work, I'm being offered a slot in the popular crowd.

I look from Paige to Carmen to Wendy. This is my chance. These girls could be my new best friends. I could be where I belong.

But in my gut, I'm not sure I *do* belong in their crowd. After everything that's happened in the last twenty-four hours — after everything I've been through with Sasha and Marc — something has changed.

I glance at Sasha, and I realize that she's been a better friend to me than Paige could probably ever be. Sasha has been nothing but kind to me, while Paige and her group have pretty much been nothing but mean. Until now. But there's no guarantee their sweetness will last. I know that well enough from my friends back home.

"Thanks, but I don't think I can make it tonight," I tell Paige, and her mouth falls open in shock. This must be the first time anyone has ever turned her down. "I'm pretty beat, so I'd rather do something low-key." I glance at Sasha. "Maybe we could get In-N-Out burgers and fries and go back to your house?"

Sasha grins at me. "Sounds fab."

"Fine," Paige sniffs, tossing her hair over her shoulder. "Your loss. See you around, Ashlee. Sasha." She nods curtly at us, then marches off, Carmen and Wendy trailing after her.

"What happened to you?" Sasha asks me. "I thought you'd be all over that party."

"I don't know. Maybe you misjudged me," I reply, echoing Paige.

Sasha throws her head back and laughs. I start laughing, too. Something about Sasha's attitude — her loudness, even her wild clothes — is freeing and fun.

Right then, Marc comes up to us, his eyes sparkling.

"Rumor has it that Ms. Anderson is about to take a cast and crew photo," he says. He nods toward the cookie table, where the cast members have started grouping together.

"I'm way ahead of you," Sasha says, elbowing Marc in the ribs. "I told Ashlee that you guys need to hide out or something."

"Let's chill by the punch table," Marc suggests. "They won't miss us. Meanwhile, you go get 'em, superstar," he tells Sasha, giving her a gentle shove.

She sticks her tongue out at him but scurries off.

"Good plan," I tell Marc, skirting behind a wall of people so that we're more or less out of sight. I pour us each a glass of cranberry juice. It's not Sanga!, but it'll do.

"Hey, you're the one with the good plans," he replies, accepting the cup from me. "Seriously, Ashlee," he says, his brown eyes sincere. "I think it's awesome how you figured out that Mr. Harker was the Dark One. Not to mention how you came up with that idea to trap him. You're really smart, you know?"

"Oh . . . um, thanks," I say, glancing down and blushing furiously.

Back in New York, a couple boys had told me I was pretty, but no one had ever said I was smart. Which means a whole lot more. And the fact that Marc is the one to say it now makes my whole chest expand and contract. Kind of like my heart is bursting.

"I couldn't have done it without you," I tell him honestly.

"Cheers," he says, lifting his cranberry juice. As we tap our cups together, I finally admit it to myself: I may have a tiny, sort-of crush on Marc. I'm not sure if he feels the same way about me, but I do remember something Sasha said, back when I first became wardrobe master. *"I bet a certain someone will be glad about that."* Had she meant Marc? Had her brother said something about me?

I'll have to ask Sasha later, when the time is right.

"Look, they're taking the photo," Marc says, pointing through the crowd. "I'm glad they forgot about us."

I stand on my toes to see, but then my phone buzzes in the pocket of my black pants. I take it out and read the text:

Hope the play went well! Call u tomorrow! XOXO Eve & Mal

I smile. I'm not sure if I'll ever be as close to my New York City girls as I once was, but I know we'll always be friends. And I have new friends here.

I gaze around the cafeteria. The cast and crew are clustered together, making goofy poses as Ms. Anderson snaps their photo. Arabella and Beau are getting autographs from Mr. Hirsh, and Mom, Dylan, and Diana are all talking with Nurse Murray. The air in the room smells like sugar and punch. Outside, I know, the palm trees are swaying in the wind and the ocean waves are crashing against the shore.

Tomorrow, maybe, I'll bat-shift out of the blue again. Or get annoyed at Dylan. Or worry that my mom will catch me drinking Sanga! That's tomorrow, though.

Life isn't always perfect, after all. But tonight, at least, it feels pretty close.

BITE INTO ANOTHER POISON APPLE, IF YOU DARE...

The bat on the windowsill began to transform. The wings disappeared and were replaced by long, graceful arms. The squat, furry body lengthened out and began to take on a human form. As I stared, my eyes growing wider, my pulse pounding at my throat, the big bat ears shrunk. Then, the tiny bat head began to morph into a human face. A *familiar* human face.

The face of Great-aunt Margo.

I clapped my hand over my mouth to silence my scream. All I wanted to do was run, but my legs wouldn't work.

Please let this be one of those nightmares, I prayed over and over. *Please let Mom call my name. Please let me wake up in my bed.*

But I didn't wake up. I stood there, trembling from head to toe. Finally, I was able to move. I spun around and tore toward my bedroom. With quivering hands, I shut the door and flung myself onto my bed, burrowing under my covers and trying to stop my teeth from chattering.

Did I really see that? Am I going crazy? My mind was racing as fast as my heart.

I drew my knees to my chest and sat still in the darkness while the storm raged outside. All my life, I'd suspected that there were secrets lurking behind the ordinary, that there was more to reality than met the eye. And now, I had actual evidence.

The realization struck me all at once, as fast as a flash of lightning. It was so crazy, but so obvious that I couldn't deny it.

My great-aunt was a lot more than just weird.

She was a vampire.

POISON APPLE BOOKS

The Dead End

This Totally Bites!

Miss Fortune

Now You See Me...

Midnight Howl

Her Evil Twin

Curiosity Killed the Cat

At First Bite

THRILLING.

BONE-CHILLING.

THESE BOOKS

HAVE BITE!

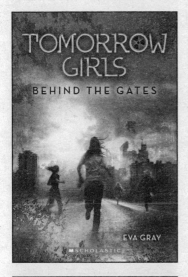

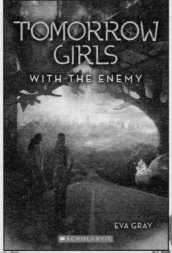
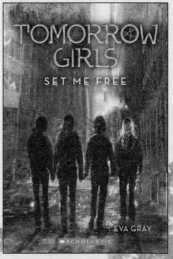

Petal Pushers

Four sisters. One flower shop.
Will disaster bloom?

Don't miss any of these fresh, sweet reads!